"These stories are *hot*
and the sheer beaut*
and better."
—Miciah Bay Gault, author of *Goodnight Stranger*

"Open this book to any page—you can't lose. *All Daughters Are Awesome Everywhere* is indeed awesome on every page. These meticulously detailed stories earned both my admiration and love. Great reading experience."
—Rion Amilcar Scott, author of *The World Doesn't Require You*

"In *All Daughters Are Awesome Everywhere* DeMisty D. Bellinger has gifted us a book of many worlds beneath the same roof, its stories and characters at turns brash, tender, joyous, sly, and always deeply, messily human. I loved dwelling in these pages. I loved the ride this collection took me on: one full of surprises and heart."
—emily m. danforth, author of *Plain Bad Heroines* and *The Miseducation of Cameron Post*

"The stories in *All Daughters Are Awesome Everywhere* are a lesson in creative risk-taking. With this bold collection of genre-bending tales, Bellinger invites us to dismantle binaries around sexuality and gender, grief and comfort, desire and repulsion, damnation and redemption in ways that challenge and champion the messy mystery that is the human heart."
—Sheree L. Greer, author of *Once and Future Lovers: Tenth Anniversary Edition*

"Infectious reading. *All Daughters Are Awesome Everywhere* is a feast of storytelling where women—mothers, daughters, and lovers—travel the roads between a world that wishes to constrain them and the ferocious realm of their own desires."
—Elwin Cotman, author of *Weird Black Girls*

All Daughters Are
Awesome Everywhere

ZERO STREET FICTION   *Series Editors*
Timothy Schaffert
SJ Sindu

All DAUGHTERS Are AWESOME EVERYWHERE

STORIES

DeMisty D. Bellinger

University of Nebraska Press
LINCOLN

Acknowledgments for the use of previously
published material appear on pages ix–x, which
constitute an extension of the copyright page.

The University of Nebraska Press is part
of a land-grant institution with campuses
and programs on the past, present, and
future homelands of the Pawnee, Ponca,
Otoe-Missouria, Omaha, Dakota, Lakota,
Kaw, Cheyenne, and Arapaho Peoples, as
well as those of the relocated Ho-Chunk,
Sac and Fox, and Iowa Peoples.

Library of Congress
Cataloging-in-Publication Data
Names: Bellinger, DeMisty D., author.
Title: All daughters are awesome everywhere:
stories / DeMisty D. Bellinger.
Description: Lincoln: University of Nebraska
Press, 2024. | Series: Zero Street fiction
Identifiers: LCCN 2024002483
ISBN 9781496241306 (paperback)
ISBN 9781496241658 (epub)
ISBN 9781496241665 (pdf)
Subjects: BISAC: FICTION / LGBTQ+ / General |
FICTION / Literary | LCGFT: Short stories.
Classification: LCC PS3602.E45775 A45
2024 | DDC 813/.6—dc23/eng/20240119
LC record available at
https://lccn.loc.gov/2024002483

Designed and set in Adobe Jensen by N. Putens.

For Marlena and Anaïs, who fill me with wonder every day.

CONTENTS

ACKNOWLEDGMENTS

Thank you to Timothy Schaffert, SJ Sindu, Alice Tasman, Judith Slater, Hannah Grieco, Leesa Cross-Smith, Hannah Cohen, Rion Amilcar Scott, Meagan Lucas, Jericho Brown (you may not remember, but you encouraged and inspired a short story), Laura Pegram, Chaya Bhuvaneswar, Eric and Genevieve, Ianna Small, Troy Palmer, Terry Burns, Russ Brickey, Kara Candito, Tony Bouxa, Matt Hart, Michael Hammerle, and Kathleeen Driskell. I'm forgetting people, I know. Also, thanks to the folks at Fitchburg State University, especially the English Studies Department, and to Hildy Schilling and Sean Goodlett, just for your friendship and support.

Maxine and Laurence, my parents, have always encouraged me to reach for the stars, and I am forever grateful. And thanks to Neal, always, first reader, best friend.

The following stories have been previously published: "Black Girl's Magic" in *Cotton Xenomorph*; "Acquiring Joshua" in *Specter Magazine*; "A Lost Day" in *Barren Magazine*; "Love Your Braider" in

Prairie Wolf Press Review; "Awesome Everywhere" in *Kweli Journal*; "Jubilee" as "Palladia" in *Kalyani Magazine*; "Tiger-Free Days" in *WhiskeyPaper* and *Fractured Lit*; "Ballad of Jane" in *Helen Literary Magazine*; "Free Fish" in *Good River Review*; "Cat, Catfish, Cat" in an earlier form in *Necessary Fiction* and *Women's Anthology: Carrying Fire*; "Ladybird, Ladybird" in *Okay Donkey* and *Middle House Review*; "Whisper Network" in *midnight & indigo*; "The Ballad of Frankie Baker" in *Little Fiction | Big Truths* and *The Best Small Fictions 2019*; "Going Home" as "Fly Away Home" in *Forklift, Ohio*; "The Negotiation of Space" in *Driftless Review* and *Derelict Lit*; "French Fry Soup" in *WhiskeyPaper*; "Good Fit" in *Porcupine Literary*; "All the Dreams You've Yet to Have" in *Middle House Review*; "An Opossum Tale" in *Good River Review*.

All Daughters Are
Awesome Everywhere

PART I

Alice was not much surprised
at this, she was getting so used
to queer things happening.

—LEWIS CAROLL,
Alice in Wonderland

Black Girl's Magic

VOODOO DOLL

She calls me her voodoo doll and sticks a sewing needle in the fattest part of my left breast. I am surprised at how much it hurts, how much it feels good, and wonder if there's blood. "Hold still, now," she says, "for it to work. Close your eyes and channel your energy through the needle." She stabs another needle, this time my right arm, the shoulder. How many more times she'll jab me? How did we get here, me letting her pincushion me? And who, I wondered, was she directing this pain to? Who was on the other side?

ZOMBIED

I think I'm high, but I don't remember smoking or drinking anything. I look in the mirror to check if my eyes are bloodshot, and they're not; they are typing paper white. My skin is discolored with white powder, and I can see my brown hues hidden beneath. I think: white face. I think: I must go pull the weeds, mow the lawn, take out the garbage, and cut the stems from the greens.

READ ME

The snake was disorienting. I kept my eyes on him (his name was Baby Legba), even as she wrapped him around me, erasing the negative energy, centering me. The snake and the fifty candles brought me somewhere else. I sat down, cross-legged on the floor, across from her. Her hazel eyes transported me. The bones, cowry shells, and crystals she shook hypnotized me. "Ask your question," she said, "in your head." Baby Legba hissed a whisper hiss, then slithered away into a corner, coiled up. She threw the pieces in her hands onto the marked floor between us. The bones and crystals so polished, they collected all of the light from the fifty candles and from the fire of her hazel eyes.

PRAYER

Before we go to bed, she feeds flower petals to a shrine. She gets on her knees and says the Lord's Prayer, then reads her rosary. She sprinkles the room with blessed water. She asks me when I am going to pray, and I shrug. She cuts her eyes at me and says, "You have to live a spiritual life." I say, "I believe in you." She looks even angrier and begins to peel away her clothes. I follow suit and ask if she'll still have me over. "Don't be foolish," she says.

BEFORE MORNING

in that liminal period when the moon is still setting and the sun is still rising, you are up sprinkling your deck with watered-down rum. I feel heavy and stay in your bed, watching the day changing out your window. Then I remember Baby Legba, and I sit straight up. You come back to bed and smile at me. "He's in a terrarium," you say. "You're safe. You're always safe." You kneel beside the mattress and say a silent prayer. I fall back to sleep and offer potential nightmares to the fading moonlight.

SUNDAY MORNING

Before church, we eat a simple meal of grits and fried eggs. I cook. She prefers her egg poached, and I prefer scrambled. We eat in silence. When she finishes, she asks me how I'm liking my visit. I don't tell her that I would like to have sex with her. Instead, I ask, "Where was all this in college?" "Hidden," she says. She doesn't have to explain what I already know about hiding, about keeping secrets that you share with only yourself and those who came before you. This is the Black girl magic we all inherently know, the gris-gris we intrinsically carry within ourselves, a protection we depend on.

Before we go, she tells me, she will let herself be possessed. "It may look scary, but it won't be. It may seem like a celebration, and it will be. Sort of. A couple of guys will be here soon." And there isn't a knock on the door but an opening up of the door. Men with drums. She puts on more beads. The men begin pounding their instruments and singing. They move with the rhythm they create. She, too, sways, then dances. Her eyes go white. I start thinking about mowing the lawn, and I start thinking about the needles. What had happened?

(Sunday Morning: Later)

A transformation. Sunday best and reserved demeanor. The singing is only of hymns. The rhythm only in melody. And be with you. And God be with you. Amen.

SUNDAY NIGHT

After her rosary, she tells me that none of it is learned. "No one would teach me. Instead, I gleaned what I could from watching my grandmother and aunts. Mama wanted no part of it. And Daddy, well, he's white. Nothing wrong with being white, but, well." I reach out to her and take her hands. There is a place between all of this where Western sin doesn't exist and I could kiss her. I could lie back and have her insert me with needles. Where I could feel the surprising heat of melting wax from prayer candles. But the burn isn't really surprising, right? So why do I jump? Why do I flinch?

MONDAY

Again, a transformation. She's in business casual and straightened hair. I'm packed and going back home to a husband who is as tired as cynicism. Tired as in: I'm tired of him. Tired as in: we're tired together. Our children only interested in what is projected. I could show them the world in the sunlight, but they'd reach back to be inside. She pulls in front of my terminal entrance at the airport. "Life isn't fun there," I say. "My life ain't fun either. You only see the exciting parts." I kiss her again, once more until next year. "God be with you," she says. "Goodbye," I say.

Acquiring Joshua

She had started spreading over to Joshua's side of the bedroom. A little at first: a pair of earrings one day, a compact mirror and a couple of business cards she collected the next day. Once, he'd come home to find her horizontally on the bed, one arm on his pillow. Her panties and pantyhose were on his side of the floor. Her blazer draped over his chair. Monday morning, he found that his men's size eleven feet fit comfortably inside of her women's size seven shoes, which he found beneath his side of the bed where his Top-Siders should have been. With no other shoes nearby, he wore them to work. He marveled at the height they gave him, how the heel points made him walk straight—his back a perfectly erect T and his feet following one in front of the other with each step. People noticed him that day. Stood when he entered the room. They answered his questions and fulfilled his requests immediately.

Thursday, at 11:22 a.m., he was in the bathroom reapplying a coat of raisin-red lipstick. Peterson was in the bathroom, too, and watched him don it. "Looking good, Joshua."

"Thanks."

"You know, Rogers is retiring. You should go up for his position. Time you made vice president of something, right? Only one way to go, Joshua. Don't think about the other way."

That night over dinner, he noticed his wife's five o'clock shadow. She ate a burger and a half with two servings of mashed potatoes and a huge salad. Joshua had the salad and the burger patty, no bun.

His wife dropped him off at work. She wore a tie that could be considered spiffy. He recognized the tie. "I bought this for you," she said. He smiled and fingered the buttons on her shirt. "Going up for this promotion," Joshua said, "makes me hot."

He wore an Anne Taylor suit with a cute satin extension at the hem. Gold earrings with tear-shaped pearls dangled from both lobes. He tried not to, but he kept playing with the charm around his neck during the interview, but the board loved all his answers. "It would be nice," he heard Peterson say, "if we could get some diversity in the upper ranks, right gentlemen?"

That night Joshua and his wife made love. When they finished, they could not separate. "It's our love," Joshua said. "I love you so much." The epiphany made him weep. He felt his wife's vagina envelop him more, and instead of going flaccid, he grew into her.

"It'll be hard to go to work," he said.

"We'll go to work," she said. "You worry so much over everything."

Sunday, at church, Joshua felt a kid's eyes on them. A kid of five or maybe six years old. He couldn't help but to feel judged by this child, a dark-haired boy with dark eyes, lashes long as falsies. Joshua scratched above his left ear, but found his wife's cheek there instead, which was slightly fuzzy even though she had shaved. He realized he hadn't shaved his own face in a week, but he had shaved his legs and armpits. The hair in these places, though, thinned considerably.

He saw the child's mother admonish the child for staring. He read the word *abomination* on her lips. He thought that they should go, that he didn't feel comfortable in the church. He wanted to tell his wife that they should leave, but she already knew. They rose together. They talked as they walked out, not saying a word aloud but saying, to each other, how alone they felt from that world inside the church and that condemning word.

"There is always work," he said aloud once they were outside. "They like me at work."

His wife tried reaching into her pocket for the car keys but instead grabbed their penis, which was where her right pocket would have been.

"Here," he said. He put his free hand around her shoulder and pulled her closer to him. She pushed into him. The sensation was similar to unpleasant but obligatory sex.

"How do you think we look?" his wife asked. "Like how our child would look," he said. "We can never kiss again," someone said. "We are kissing all the time," someone said.

Dreams Formed in Rain

A chance of rain presents in a reality of a hailstorm, replete with lightning. Joie wonders how her oldest, Madeline, is fairing in kindergarten. Carlos, now on floor time, starts screaming when thunder peals throughout the neighborhood. And the littlest, Freda, was at Joie's breast, suckling slowing and falling asleep. Joie worried about the car—the good car—left outside of the garage so she could quickly load it up with Carlos, Freda, diaper bag, backpack, purse, and bottles of water and pumped milk and cow's milk and dammit do not forget the phone again when she would have to leave in about a half hour to pick up Madeline from school.

Again, attachment parenting felt like a trap.

Joie looked out the window from where she sat on the floor, near newly crawling Carlos crying about the loud noises from the world outside, and saw pea-sized hail falling on the hood of the good car.

Could she, Joie wondered, put the baby down and trust that Carlos would be okay with his extended floor time and the thunder and lightning and the hail plinking the house and the patio, run out, park the car in the garage quickly, and run back in to check on the baby and Carlos? Hopefully, in that time the kids wouldn't get into any trouble.

Could she just run out to the car and drive in the hailstorm sans the baby or the toddler and let the kindergartener get picked up by Bobby when he's done at work? And where would she drive to?

Years ago, before Bobby, before the concept of attachment parenting, before the idea of working at home, there was Nebraska and there was Sarah. Sarah's skin was the color of parchment paper, her Afro red and fuzzy, her nose and high cheekbones dotted with freckles that brought out the impossible hazel of her eyes. Sarah and Joie ran to Joie's car, an old Monte Carlo with two-tone doors and roof. Joie loved that car, and although the hail in Nebraska was unbelievably large, literally golf ball sized, making violent noises as it crashed on the springtime earth, the unassuming building structures, and the other cars parked around them. When she said goodbye to Sarah and the thrill of the Monte Carlo, there were three dents in the hood of the car, as if a strong toddler had punched the car in a tantrum. Where was Sarah now? "Vegas, baby!"

She had said that she was moving to Las Vegas, and last they checked in, Sarah still had the car but hardly drove it. It was still dented. And Joie never visited.

Joie could, theoretically, leave Freda and Carlos and GPS her way to Nevada. Surely, Bobby could understand that she had a life before Madeline and him, a life where she lived Sundays with a mixture of equal parts trepidation and optimistic anticipation. Now she dreaded Mondays because she would be at home, attached to two or three children, depending on the hour of the day.

Carlos's sobbing grew with the fall of the hail, and unlike other New England hailstorms, which were rare as albino deer, this storm intensified as the minutes wore on, not growing in size but definitely accelerating. More thunder, more lightning, and Joie put the baby down. Next to Carlos. Without raincoat or umbrella, without a proper pair of shoes, Joie slipped out in her well-worn flip-flops, car keys in hand, jumping slightly when the thunder struck, then lightning. Out from under the eaves and awning, she could feel the pebble-toss patter of hailstones and early-spring raindrops fall on her exposed skin and the crown of her head. She had meant to move the car, but she could not move herself. The hail was acupuncture. The hail was a bed of nails. The hail was pressure points pinning down each ache of parenthood. The rain washed away little hands, sticky with sweets and covered in dirt, constantly grabbing and clasping onto her hands, her knees, the hems of her dresses and shirts. The precipitation freed her breasts from gummy mouths sprouting ready incisors gnawing at her tender skin.

How many miles to Las Vegas? How many days and nights on the road?

But the rain and hail did something else, as did the noisy skies. Thunder sounded again, and Joie jumped. She turned toward the side window she had only a minute or two before been peering out of, to see if her kids were okay. She could see the hint of Carlos, crawling away from his sister, not crying, looking for Joie. His searching for her made Joie feel as if she was being pursued by a monster, seeing him, seeking her out. Quiet, or the monster will hear you. Still, or the ghoul will get you.

What was it that Sarah did now? A slightly bigger chunk of hail hit Joie's cheek, hard enough for it to sting, maybe hard enough for her to bleed. She remembered, then, when she was too rough with Sarah, when she had bit her lip and licked the blood that seeped from Sarah's mouth. Sex with her was always an adventure, and sex with Bobby was beginning to go stale.

What was it in Vegas? Was that what she wanted?

Another larger hail ball hit Joie's shoulder. She was here to move the car. Breaking herself out of her daydreaming. She entered the car and started it, opened the garage door. She fancied putting the car into reverse, turning out onto the road. Why Las Vegas? Wouldn't that be where they'd look?

Of course, she drove the car into the garage, cut the engine, and inhaled. Maybe another day.

A Lost Day

You have to interrupt your planned day. This is not abnormal; often things go wrong. Not just in your life but in everyone's life. Still, today was going to be the day that you master the Saint-Saëns. For once (or maybe for the third or fourth time), you were going to actually practice for four hours with little breaks in between, and maybe you were going to practice a little longer than four hours. You were going to get through the first movement of Saint-Saëns's Third Concerto with no mistakes because you only had until December, and December would be there before you know it, and that was when you'd have your first rehearsal with the entire orchestra (December 2; it was on the calendar). From memory. Or mostly memory. Eventually, you'll have everything memorized.

You were worried that the conductor for Riverwest Symphony Orchestra is too young. But what is too young? Besides, everyone has to start somewhere. And it is a community orchestra, so you consider this a way to give back to the community. And you are happy with the diversity of the orchestra. It will be the first time that you won't be the only Black musician or one of the only two Black musicians on onstage. So maybe your worrying made you distracted, or maybe it was too dry (there is nothing like the odd dryness of Wisconsin winters. Is it the weather, or is it the effect of the furnace? Whatever it is, your skin is always dry, your hair is also dry, your instrument too sharp whenever you take it out of the case), but your D string peg popped, cracked, and was finished. Fuck.

You still have your student violin. Of course, you could just use that for your four-hour session, but no. You have to interrupt your planned day. You have to pack up your violin again and take it to Lake Michigan Strings. On your way there, you almost hit the biker—and who bikes in November? In Wisconsin? You scare the biker nearly to death, then calm her down and put her in your car. And drive her to where she was going. "I'm a violinist," you say. Like she cares. Your instrument is in the trunk; she didn't have to know. But you want to impress her. You want her to know that yes, Black women can and do play classical instruments. You want her to know that you could make a living from your art. So, you lose a day.

Before you accompany her upstairs to her apartment, she asks if she could ever see your violin. You say it is broken. You open the trunk of your car and open the case, pull back the velvet and satin cover to show her. "I popped a peg," you say.

"That sounds nasty," she says.

You think about being witty by saying something like, "Well, I'm a nasty woman," but you don't. How could you even tell if she was interested? You look at her and see that, yes, she is interested.

Some time has passed, some actions were taken, and you're in her bed. Your violin is on her coffee table. She is making some Italian dish—homemade noodles and vodka sauce. She says, "I was going to make it for myself, but I have enough for two."

Soon you're eating with her and forgetting about the time. She mentions your broken violin, and you shrug. "It'll get fixed," you say, realizing that your statement sounds like fairies would come flying through her opened window (and why is her window open? It is November. In Wisconsin!) and get to work on your busted D peg.

"When do you move in?" she asks. You both laugh. And after you finish eating, you make love again. You like how she's both soft and muscular. Her belly is pudgy, and her thighs are giving, but her biceps and her calves are strong and sinewy. She smiles with her mouth closed as you kiss her neck, and when she climaxes, she's silent.

Your brain gets silly. You've got yourself attached too quickly, again. Why are you imagining a future with her? Why are you thinking about times you'll cook for her? You don't even know her taste in music. Is there someone else in her life? You don't know!

Still holding her, look at the clock. It's nearly four, and Lake Michigan Strings will be closing at five. You imagine Jack cleaning shop, finishing up a lesson or a sale, sanding down a bridge. "I should go," you say, not moving, still holding her.

"Your violin," she says. "I know. Will you invite me to the concert?" she asks.

"Of course." Maybe you should start packing your house up. Maybe you will move in.

She politely wiggles out of your arms. "What kind of music is it?"

"Art," you say, worried about *classical* getting mixed up with *Classical*, when Saint-Saëns is Romantic, and you think of saying this but remember what happened with Me'Shell, who said you were too bougie and not bohemian like she thought. But would this one—was her name actually Becky? No, it was Beth. You just called her name—be so turned off by your knowledge of art music? "Classical," you say. "He's a Romantic composer, late nineteenth, early twentieth century."

She's getting dressed without washing. That's a turnoff.

"Any composer I would have heard of?"

You get out of her bed. You look around you. "You have a towel or something? I'm going to quickly freshen up."

"Of course."

You make it to Lake Michigan Strings at 4:43 p.m. You can see Jack inside, straightening out guitars and music stands. You rush in and smile at him. "You fell in love again," he says.

"What?"

"In love. It's a long ways from spring, honey, so you can slow down with the love affairs."

"Don't call me 'honey,' Jack."

"Am I wrong?"

"It was probably just a one-night thing. Or day. Hey, you got any pegs? I'll let you call me 'honey.'"

"Let me see."

You put your case on the counter, and Jack pops it open. "Oh, honey, what did you do to Vivien this time? You torture the poor girl."

"If you don't like my playing, you can keep that shit to yourself."

"Hey, language! Children come to this establishment! Speaking of which, you need another student?"

"Maybe. Can you fix it? I need to practice for an upcoming show."

"Don't you always? I can fix it, but you're going to have to leave it here for a day. It's not just the string. Look." He shows me the scroll and points at the peg hole. He sighs heavily. You sort of see that the threading is smooth or not so smooth.

"What I'm looking at?"

"Some grooving on my part. Some sanding. And you know I have to fit the peg. You want a loaner?"

"No, I want Vivien."

"You can take her, but she won't have a D. Now I'm sure the piece you're playing needs a D." Jack takes out a cleaning cloth and wipes the other strings down.

"Just do a tune-up," you say. "All new strings, please. Check the bridge too."

"Yes, my liege." He bows slightly.

"Fuck you."

"The children!"

"Hey, Jack," you casually lean your elbow on the counter and try to look at Jack from the side of your face. The goal here is to present yourself as not really interested, not really caring. You are only making conversation. "What did you mean by saying I'm in love?"

"You want to know how I know? I ask you: am I wrong?"

You shrug. "Like I said. It was just today. I could have been here three, four, hours ago."

"But you were with her," he says. He smirks because he is so sure of himself. He unloosens the strings on your violin. "Want all new pegs? Got some ebony bitches in yesterday. Darker than you."

You roll your eyes at the casual racism. "I'm sure they're not really ebony."

"They are. I'll give the set to you for only sixty."

"You're so kind," you say and give him a sneer.

"It's that when you're dating a girl, you get this euphoric but guilty look on your face, like it's not okay to be with a woman."

"That's probably my mother looking over my shoulder."

"But clearly, you enjoy being with women. All your long-term relationships are with women."

"You're right, but that's only thus far. I am capable of falling in love with men too."

"One-day stand, huh? Did you get her number?"

"I got her everything. We're going out this Friday."

"You'd never do that with a guy."

"What do you mean?"

"Move that fast with a guy. Come back tomorrow around noon. Maybe one o'clock. I'll have your Vivien good as new."

"Let me see that loaner."

"It's special! Lock up the store, and I'll be right back."

It is five o'clock. You go to turn off the OPEN sign and flip the sign on the door over. You physically turn locks. Jack goes in the back, probably to his overstuffed office with Frankenstein projects. He left Vivien on the counter, and you go look at her. With the pegs and strings off, the bridge has slid off the body and lays beside it. She looks tragic. The shape of the violin is the shape of a woman. The real Vivien, who gave you this violin years ago, was shaped this way. You were leaving her dorm room as you had so many nights before. She stopped you and thrust the instrument toward you. She insisted you take it for keeps. "I don't play anymore," she said. "I never have the time. You are so much better on it than me, and let's face it: it's a better instrument than yours any day." She offered it three times, so you took it. You said good night and took her in your arms. You kissed her, and she kissed back, just like always, those long, sensual soft-lipped kisses.

"If you ever want it back," you said to her.

"I won't."

"I can't afford to buy this from you."

"I'm not selling it to you."

Jack returns with the loaner. You can see that it is well played. He hands it to you, and you like the heft of it. You take your own bow and rosin it up. You tune the loaner, and you are comforted by its warmness. You play your show-off piece, the Paganini, and it fills the shop with beauty. "Just a loaner, huh?"

"Only for my favorite musicians."

You play through something slow. It's no one's piece, just long notes in B-flat minor and lots of vibrato. You close your eyes against the pathos of what you're playing. You can't help but think of the girl who gave you a head start in the music world. "It's better than Vivien," you say.

Jack nods. "If you want to trade it out, just say the word."

"The woman who gave me Vivien gave all of her friends wonderful things from her closets, her drawers, her bookshelves. Then she went away. In retrospect, everything she did made sense and didn't make sense at all. I loved her very much."

You bring the violin up to your chin and drum the fingerboard. Your skin against the thread of the strings gives nearly silent intonations. It was a good instrument. "Give me a case for this one, Jack. I'll be back tomorrow."

Three Tiers of Toppings

I. THE RIGHTS OF ROBOTS

The tragedy, in spite of the tunneled ass and vagina and realistic, pliable lips, and the human-like sound of flesh when he slaps her(its) behind, or thighs, or when his body thrusts against her(its) body, was that she couldn't sigh. He couldn't catch an unintentional frown or forehead wrinkled in worry. He could not force the line of consent, see her hesitantly acquiesce to his demands, because she was only willing. He said each time a safety word, and each time she(it) would say, "Okay," in a voice breathy with desire, but she'd never use it. She would never say it.

2. DE-PRIVILEGED

She tells him his blue eyes are reminiscent of a children's pool full of piss and ants. He laughs at that, and she slaps him. He goes silent. "Call me bitch," she says. He does, and she slaps him. "Say it." He says, "Ni—," and she grabs his tie. "Bow to me," she said. "On your knees. On all fours." She straps it on and goes to work.

3. DEVOTION

"Yes" because you took the time to learn what scares me, what pains me, what pushes me, to bring me to the feathery end, then mercifully stop. "Madam" because you are quiet and kind when I'm concentrating on what it is to be loved that way. And "please" because you know, too, what thrills me, what empowers me, what makes me laugh.

Love Your Braider

Goldie was tender headed. Not only was her hair the wrong color, but it had the nerve to be nappy. It was not the texture of regular Black folks' hair but this odd, untamable mess that was almost soft, almost curly, almost *good*. It tangled in spite of a comb. She had ugly hair for a mixed woman. Goldie knew that her mother wanted a kid with long, curly, black, good hair—almost like white people's hair but more like a Puerto Rican's hair. But this is what Goldie got: coarse, curly hair with an orangey-yellowish color. Hence her name.

When Goldie's mother deemed her child old enough, she had her hair dyed black. Since then, people blamed her name on her skin tone. And when Goldie was old enough that her hair was made her own responsibility, she kept it braided and dyed black. Besides Goldie's mother, only Candance knew the color of Goldie's hair because she was the one who had dyed it for Goldie as soon as those orange-yellow roots came in. "Goldie," she'd say, "your name-sake's showing." Then Goldie'd go and buy a bottle, and Candance would dye it, which kept Goldie looking almost normal—save for the freckles and the pale skin that covered her, which made everyone ask what is she, as if she was not human but some exotic animal. The freckles, the pale skin, and the Ebonics all stretched across that broad nose made her unclassifiable.

"Ow," Goldie said when Candance dragged the comb across her head a little too roughly, trying to get the knots out before braiding the next section. Candance felt sorry for Goldie. Poor Goldie, so odd no Black man wanted her, no white man, no man. She knew that Goldie was well over thirty and had never been in a serious relationship.

"I know, girl," Candance said. "Your hair is—" she began but stopped herself. She tried to come up with a civil way of putting it. "The humidity," she said, "is really bothering your hair."

"Don't I know it," said Goldie, knowing that her hair was just nappy, humid or not. Only Goldie and her lovers knew that she had been in a couple of relationships where her partners had preferred to keep them secret. Those relationships consisted of sex she didn't enjoy, but it was nice to be with someone, even if it was just to cook for him and to clean up after him. They would watch the games on Sunday afternoons and Monday nights on her color satellite TV. Then he'd go home. Sex and service.

Once, it wasn't like that. She had been the one who kept the relationship a quiet and close little thing. She kept her mouth shut because in their neighborhood, it was taboo to be lesbian. But in that one affair, everything was shared. Food was cooked together. Lovemaking was awkward because of its newness but enjoyable because of its sincerity. It was all wonderful until the girl went away to school. She only came home holidays, and Goldie couldn't get close enough to her. She could only want the girl from afar and hug her as she would hug a friend. Then Goldie turned thirty. Then thirty-one. Aging never stops.

Goldie didn't consider herself a lesbian, though. She just considered the need to be close. To share. She didn't care who needed her.

While Goldie sat and thought of her past love life, Candance told her, "Your roots are about to grow up out this ground and start walking! I'm seeing that orange everywhere in your head."

"It is?" Goldie asked. She wasn't sure if she was ready for a dye job, or for a change. Shocking herself and her hair braider, sitting there on the porch and watching the pedestrians and the rare car go by, Goldie said, "What if I cut it?"

Candance didn't answer immediately. She finished braiding the braid she was working on and waited for Goldie to say more. When she understood that Goldie had nothing else to add, Candance asked, "What do you mean?"

"Well, let it grow, of course, until it was long enough to braid. To French braid, at least. But to let the roots grow in," she said aloud, and to herself, the idea continued: *and establish themselves, as voluntary trees would, and grow where no one treads.*

Again, Candance was silent for some time before asking, "And have yellow hair?"

Candance's heart went out to her client, but Goldie being a customer—a porch customer but a paying customer who was sure to dish out the fifty bucks flat fee plus a three-dollar tip—tried to talk her through this. Goldie was pitiful, but Candance saw her point: why should she have to dye her hair? "To make the transition easier," she said, recalling the three months she spent in cosmetology college before dropping out, "we can put in a dark rinse, like a burgundy, for a few months. Then we can cut it. Yeah, it could work."

Both women were quiet, both separately imagining Goldie with golden hair, frizzy and all about as it was meant to be. Wild. In their imaginations, they saw Goldie staring in the mirror and loving herself. They knew that her hair grew fast. It was all very possible.

Goldie said nothing but agreed to the rinse. Later she'd tell Candance to pick up whatever color she thought best from the beauty supply store, but now she leaned her cheek against Candance's thigh. It smelled of baby powder, which Candance used to keep the sweat at bay in the heat and humidity of July. Along with the powder, she wore a lotion lightly scented, one that, when emitting its aroma with the powder, reminded Goldie of her long-ago girl lover. The girl who went away to college and came home only on holidays. And Candance's skin was as soft as that girl's. The timbre of Candance's voice, which continued on about hair color, dyes, hair texture, movies, music, and television shows, anything to break the monotony of the buzzing cicadas in the trees, was reminiscent of Goldie's lover's voice. So Goldie rested easily against Candance's leg and fantasized about being in love. When Candance needed to get to the rear of her hair and Goldie had to lift her head up to let her, lift it away from the smoothness of Candance's thigh, Goldie couldn't remember if her fantasy was about her lover or about Candance or of someone else altogether.

Horse Sense

I keep thinking it's Monday, and when I realize that it's not, I catch myself, as if falling, physically stumbling while sitting down or standing still.

Getting the day wrong is disconcerting. It's akin to smelling one thing but tasting something else. Or worse, smelling nothing at all and trying to eat through that loss of sensation. This makes me remember when, years ago, my parents' friend, who was much older than them, lost his sense of smell. It unmoored me: one loses sight, loses their hearing, sure, but smell? I worried and wondered about whether all senses are subject to old age. I worried about losing the ability to touch, to feel the softness of fleece or the rough edge of cinder block. I still have those worries.

Tuesday and not Monday. I was here yesterday, and I am here today. I am filing records in a large room filled with dozens of file cabinets on tracks, each controlled by a steering wheel. Years ago, when I began here, I feared being smashed by file cabinets by some unwitting coworker, even though I was assured that would never happen. There it is: another fear. This Tuesday is a day of concern and fright. My neck feels cool, and the hairs there, the little curly ones right at the nape, tickle my skin. Once again, I worry that file cabinets on either side of me will close me in, unthinking cabinets moving without mercy, moving like boulders or spiked walls in some booby-trapped crypt. Had I lived a good life?

I want to say that my wife kisses me every morning and tells me what day it is, that she tells me what to expect at work, at home for dinner, what we'd watch that night, but I never married. I don't have a wife. At home there is only my cat and dog, neither of which can tell Monday from Wednesday because days of the week are the same to them. Maybe only Saturday and Sunday are different because those days my alarm doesn't go off. Those days I stay in bed until they get me up to feed them.

I'm sure that I am losing my sense of time, my memory. My father died years ago (Suicide? Accident? Either they could not tell or they would not tell me. I considered looking it up but stopped myself), and my mother died of heart disease before she turned eighty. No brothers, no sisters, no one in my family to say, "Remember that time when we . . . ?" I had cousins, sure, and aunts and uncles, but who of them could tell me my mind was slipping?

Had I a husband, he would let me know if I had said something before. He would say, "I know. You already told me." We would wonder together whether we've had that conversation before or not. We would ask each other, "Remember that time when . . . ?"

I am over forty, and I am still a file clerk. I've been here for four years because I appreciate not looking for another job. My friend Chris tells me that I need to apply myself and work someplace else. "You got a college degree," they say. "You can do a fuck ton more than filing folders." But I find joy in this comfort of not moving to another job.

I find comfort in the job itself: quietly grasping file folders, hearing them whisper softly when one cover slides against another cover, the way they always feel room temperature cool, the smoothness of their surfaces. I like finding the right section, the right alphabetical area, the right letter-number combination for the files. I like that I spend hours without seeing a colleague on some days.

I like the sighting of the rare mouse, making their way through shelving and papers.

One time I saw a pigeon and two sparrows. Had they come in together? Did they want to get out? One time: a squirrel. Hunched over, eyes wide, body still, fur rising and falling with its rapid breaths.

Chris massages my temples. They tell me not to worry about the moving files. "Don't fret over anything," they say. "You're just over forty."

"You don't think I could have Alzheimer's?" They don't say anything, but they keep rubbing my temples. They move their strong hands to my back and dig out knots with their thumbs. I slowly lean my head over until my cheek touches their bare thigh. I want to ask them to let me make love to them again, but I am afraid. "I am always afraid," I say aloud. They say they know.

After the one time, when we were intimate, they told me that I didn't love them, that we were just lonely, both of us. "We will find men again soon," they said. I reminded them that I also dated women.

Now Chris asks, "What is your earliest memory?"

I think back, and all I can imagine was preschool. "Eating paste with Jimmy Robinson and Tiffany. I don't remember Tiffany's last name."

"Tell me about the paste."

"Lumpy, sweet, the way I imagined togetherness would taste. Gooey. Later I learned that it was nontoxic, probably just flour and water, but then I knew I was doing something wrong, and that knowledge was exhilarating."

"Tell me your most recent memory."

"You rubbing my temples. Me at work trying to find the spot for the 32 Wines Restaurant files. The smell of new manila folders."

"You are not senile," my friend says. "You should have the common fucking sense to know that. The horse sense. You remember that saying? Our parents used it."

I nod. Chris says: "Tell me what you don't want to remember."

I turn and smile at them.

Brother Charlie's Intended

God bless us, we are all good Christians with traditional beliefs: no sex before marriage, no abortions, no celebrating Halloween without praising God, and Jesus Christ in all His glory, no gay sex. So imagine my absolute joy when my brother Deacon Charles Robertson III had found an equally God-fearing wife with processed, pomaded hair to wed and bed in the name of all that was holy, then be fruitful, etc., etc. I was invited to a week of: engagement party (Tuesday, June 10), the shower (Thursday, June 12; they were moving fast), the rehearsal dinner (Saturday, June 14), and the wedding (Monday, June 16).

"But I cannot attend," I emailed my mother.

She called my phone: "What do you mean 'you can't attend'? What is so important that you're going to miss your older brother's wedding? You a teacher; you have summers off."

"I am a professor, not a teacher. But I'm an artist, too, Mama, and this is the time that I create."

"Lord, do you hear this? Your brother's only getting married once!"

"Yep, just like Donnie, right?" My brother Donnie married twice.

"Are you jealous because it's not you? You are twenty-seven years old. What are you waiting for?"

God, bless us all. "Is she pregnant?"

"What?"

"Charles's intended. Why is everything so rush-rush, huh?"

"Yolanda, just come and support your brother."

"I'll see what I can do."

"Yolanda Robertson, you will be here!"

Of course, I was. With rainbow-colored bells on. I didn't tell them as much, but they should have gotten the point. Besides, I was happy for my brother. He wasn't the brightest or most handsome out of the seven of us, and I had sincerely worried that he wouldn't be partnered up because that was important to the Robertsons.

I offended easily and bristled at stereotypes or assumed expectations. I always rocked rainbow for Pride celebrations, but I wouldn't be caught dead in the bright colors regularly. I didn't care about the studies—I didn't believe in gaydar. Still, when I met my future sister-in-law Neona, I knew she wasn't with my brother because of true love. I wasn't even sure if it was a cursory adoration between the two. But what gave it away? Was it her slim figure and perky chest? Was it her smooth, cocoa-colored skin, seemingly blemish free? Was it that she did not wear her hair processed and pomaded—not to say that some gay or bisexual women didn't process their hair, but no one in our church showed up Sundays with nappy updos—or her huge hooped earrings? I saw her, and I was a believer!

"You're Charles's younger sister?" she asked.

I nodded. "I'm Yolanda." I smiled at her like I smiled at every woman who I was interested in. She smiled back, and I realized then: she didn't know she wasn't really into men. She had never entertained the thought. Or maybe she had but prayed it away. I nodded at her and took my place at the dinner table. I lamented that I couldn't tell her how I was reading the situation.

I watched my brother and this woman at the engagement party. They hardly touched. Barely looked at each other. Maybe it was the lack of lust or maybe it was the overabundance of nerves. Maybe it was my assumption, and I would swear on our family's Bible that she cut eyes at me more than once during the party.

Later that night, alone in my childhood bed, I thought about the moment in the restaurant bathroom when I saw a flash of Neona's thigh. She was fixing her skirt, and I was washing my hands. I saw more than I should have. I couldn't help but let my mind wander over her, up her inner thigh, imagine how soft her skin was, how pliant her labia. I masturbated with that image, finishing with her name on my lips.

The next day, during the gift giving segment of the wedding shower, someone gave Neona a small, fleur-de-lis-shaped vibrator. "Some people need the extra help," the well-meaning gift giver said. "I mean, you use it with your husband, not alone."

"So no masturbating, huh?" I said.

"Yolanda, that is having sex with the Devil!" my mother said. The Devil is a mighty fine lay, I thought.

"Some women," the giver said, "may not get the complete pleasure sex is supposed to give, so her husband can take this and rub it, you know, above your opening."

"And some men," another one of Neona's friends said, "like it rubbed against them. You know, like along their behind." This dark-skinned friend's face flushed red.

That was my cue to leave, if only for a minute. I stood as quietly as I could and left. I wandered outside, onto the porch, wishing I was somewhere that vibrators weren't mysterious objects. I scrolled through the news on my phone to kill time. I was engrossed with a story when I heard the back door to the house open, slam shut. Then I heard a sob. "Neona," I said. I quit the porch, walked around to the back of the house, and found my future sister-in-law.

Sure enough, she was crying. "I know how to use a vibrator," she said in a whisper.

I took her elbow. "Walk with me." She let me lead her to the alleys behind the houses, where seedy things happened. We didn't get far until we stopped on the car-width strip of road, backs of houses to us, garages. "I love my brother, but you don't have to marry him."

"I'll marry him because that is what we do." She let go of my elbow and let her fingers smooth the skin down my arm. She took my hand and turned to me. "I just want to kiss you once."

I wanted to say something witty. I wanted to tell her that she could kiss me anytime, that she could do more to me. Instead, I tried to show her what I wanted to say. I kissed her like I knew my brother never would.

PART II

If I should take a notion
To jump into the ocean,
It ain't nobody's business if I do.

—PORTER GRAINGER AND EVERETT ROBBINS,
"T'ain't Nobody's Business (If I Do)"

Awesome Everywhere

When you killed yourself, everything stopped and kept going, and that mixture of inertia and constant motion sent me reeling.

We debated, briefly, if Shelly should still perform in the final night of *Bye Bye Birdie*, but it was her second play and her first lead and she wanted to, and I wanted her to, and they rewrote the program for that night to add your name and a little tribute to what you've done for the school, the theater department, and for Shelly, and they dedicated that performance to you. Shelly got enough roses to open a flower shop. You know and I know she cannot stand pollen. But it was okay.

And life kept going on, as everyone insinuated that it would and as I knew it would. Wake, funeral, interring, repast, leftover casseroles, all that shit. I returned to work, and everyone looked sorry. Their pasty winter faces folded down in something like residual grief, and it turned my stomach so that I couldn't eat lunch. Instead, I masturbated in the handicap stall of the bathroom, and I didn't even feel guilty for doing it. I just sat there on the toilet, my winter-weight tights coiled around my ankles, my vagina sore from plunging in while dry. And I made spit bubbles, sitting there, refusing to think of you.

When Shelly was done with school for the year, I took a leave of absence from work, and we took a road trip. I made plans as we went, and I suppose I wanted to keep going, but in early August, Shelly begged to go back home. Back in Massachusetts, I returned to work for a week, but then I quit my job in September to volunteer for a political campaign. I attended rallies and went door to door for two months to persuade people to vote. When my candidate lost in November, everything felt hopeless, and I didn't know what to do.

Shelly got into that year's musical, *Into the Woods*. She had wanted the role of Little Red Riding Hood or The Witch, and she got The Witch. "It's because of my hair," she said, and I nodded in agreement. "Mr. Kinsey said he could have cast me as The Baker's Wife, but he said he wanted me on stage more, leading the search."

"The search?"

"I send people on quests into the woods to get what they wish for, but they should be careful what they wish for. Or so it goes in the play. I love Sondheim."

"Sounds interesting. Good witch?"

"Not really. She's complicated. It's a little racy too."

"Do you want me to help at all?"

She shook her head no. I suppose, what could I do to help? You were the artistic one. You helped with set design. I always stayed out of the way until opening night and disappeared again until the last show. But this time I didn't want to be alone or idle, so I kept myself busy by going to her rehearsals. And I started smoking again. I'd sit in the nearly empty high school auditorium and watch the students run lines and find their places. I would listen to the director carefully tell the high schoolers how horrible they were at acting, at singing, at dancing, at feigning love. I'd go out and smoke whatever pack of cigarettes I happened to pick up that day, because I hadn't set on a brand yet, and another mother would come out and smoke with me and tell me about how awesome her kids were as if Shelly were a piece of shit. But I told myself that Shelly was not a piece of shit and this woman didn't think that; it's just that everyone's kid is the best kid in the world.

The third day of rehearsals, she asked, "Which one is yours?"

"The tall one with all the curly hair."

She nodded, blowing smoke out at the same time. "The lead girl?" She looked disappointed. I wanted to make her hurt more.

"The lead again. She was lead last year," I said. "Yes, that's her."

"Her dad?" she started. I turned on my toes, like doing the twist. I said, "She's not a good dancer. It's not her only flaw, right? We all have many. But it hurts her in musical theater."

"Your daughter's awesome."

"That's true." I said. "All daughters are awesome everywhere."

Shelly would look at me from the corner of her eye. She never sat next to me. We hardly talked. Once she asked me, nearly October, "Why can't you be still?"

I stopped what I was doing. I wasn't still. I was sitting on the couch with crossed legs, shaking one leg as if I were rocking a baby, flicking some French rose-flavored cigarette in the ashtray I held in my other hand, bobbing my head slowly, and I'd had only sat down. But I stopped and asked, "What do you mean?"

"You're constantly moving. Since Dad died, you can't stay still. And you're always looking around you like you're some kind of cokehead or meth patient. Perpetual motion woman."

In anger I stood, upending the ashtray to the floor and spilling pastel-colored cigarette butts and fancy French ashes on the rug, the ashtray thumping like a head hitting something stationary.

I had a raised hand to, what? I would never hit Shelly. "Perpetual motion mama," I said.

I let Shelly have a Halloween party. Her fellow theater students came in intricate costumes worthy of Hollywood. There were about twenty kids, three mothers, one father, and me. The adults had beers and Bloody Marys. The kids had punch and caffeine. We had scary-themed food. I made sure everyone was comfortable—I was making sure—and Shelly told me to be still. "I got it," she said. "Me and Val," Valencia or something, "we're the hosts."

"Your daughter's beautiful," one of the mothers said to me. Shelly was beautiful. Tall and thin with small breasts and hips. Her hair lit around her like a bush fire in unkempt coils. She looked like something not quite me, not quite you. I leaned back against the wall and watched Shelly bounce around from kid to kid, entertaining, constantly entertaining.

"I'm sorry," the mother said, "for what happened."

I nodded. The apologies, nearly a year later, came yet. I closed my eyes and tried to still myself, as my daughter requested I do. I took a gulp of Bloody Mary and let the tomato pulp roll over my tongue, sludge down my throat. I let it like lava warm me beyond warm, too much. I kept drinking. When I opened my eyes again, glowing but tired kids in makeup and costume were bidding Shelly goodbye and thanking her for the party. One of the fathers was making out with one of the mothers. The other two mothers were in deep conversation. Soon Shelly was in front of me. She kind of hugged me. "Thanks, Mom," she said. She had been so cold to me, for months, cool as a vodka ad, and I fell into her hug. I glommed on.

"Mrs. McGinty? Are you going to be okay?" I looked at Val, who asked the question, and shook my head a little. I was crying.

"I think I drank too much," I said. And you had killed yourself. I was drunk, and you were dead. One of the mothers must have helped me upstairs because when I woke up, she was still there, staring at me and stroking my cheek. I jerked a little, and she didn't change what she was doing.

"How embarrassing for Shelly," I said.

"She's fine."

"Who are you?"

She leaned in and kissed my head. It felt maternal, and I felt okay about it. I grinned a little at her in thanks for her comfort, and she kissed me on the mouth. I kissed back. "I'm sorry," she said. I didn't say anything. I sat up. My brain seemed to rush into the front part of my head, where this mother had kissed me, and concentrate on an evil spot of pressure.

"Where is Shelly?" I asked.

"In her room."

"And is he still president?"

She smiled at me. "I should go."

"Did you vote for him? It's okay if you did. I don't want you to go yet. I don't want you to, you know—I'm not gay. And I don't think there's anything wrong with being gay!"

"It's fine."

"But I don't want you to go."

"I won't go. I'm Tonya's mother. We've talked about her? We smoke together at rehearsal."

"Is she still here too?"

"She, Val, and your Shelly are all downstairs."

"Then you'll stay for breakfast." I reached over and took her hand. It was not as smooth as a woman's hand should be. Clearly, she washed dishes and did other things. She said that she was a hairdresser, I believe, in one of our conversations outside of the school's theater. I imagined, even in gloves, chemicals seeping into the pores of her skin, roughening her hands in some places, smoothing them in others. "I want you to kiss me again."

Tonya's mother kissed me again, and my whole body stirred. "I still don't know your name. I should, right? We've talked so often. Here, my name is Aiesha."

She smiled.

"Delirium tremors," I said. "Is that the term? Am I hallucinating?"

"I don't know what you mean. I'm Minnie. Like the mouse."

"The mouse. How's Mickey? Would he mind us making out?"

"Mickey is actually named Jeffrey. And he is an asshole."

I called our new arrangement makeshift. Tonya slept on the couch, Minnie slept with me, and Shelly skulked everywhere in the house, but mostly in her room. She looked at me whenever we met as if she hated me. Sometimes I would try to touch her, and she would always flinch away. I chose to act as if it were always this way. Shelly chose something else.

And I couldn't get a read on Tonya for anything. She was an elusive child who spewed all her energy on the stage, and at our makeshift home, she'd close up and look around for a dark corner. Honestly, I didn't care too much because she wasn't my child, but I worried that if Tonya wasn't happy, Minnie would leave.

None of this was simple. Jeffrey, Minnie's husband, often came and yelled through the walls, threatening us with cops and social workers, saying that he wanted Tonya back. He'd call Minnie a dyke, a butch, a cunt cruncher, a whore, and me a homewrecker, a desperate widow, confused. Sometimes he'd get in, and we'd have to physically work to get him out, Minnie and me. When that happened, Tonya and Shelly would watch and wait, wanting him to go away and for Tonya and Minnie to leave with them. "You're my wife, Minnie," he'd say. "Why are you here? Your son's still home. What about him?"

Also, I don't think Shelly and Tonya liked each other. They didn't dislike each other, but they weren't friends. Our arrangement forced them together in a way that they were both uncomfortable with. They were cordial. I did see that they did not appreciate what was happening, but I enjoyed having Minnie so close to me.

And Minnie cried in her sleep. When it happened, I would lightly stroke her back and her hair. I'd kiss her awake and tell her that everything was okay and will be okay. It was late November and late at night when I finally asked about her son who was still at home with his father. We were in bed, and I knew she was awake because she kept shifting positions next to me. "Is he in high school too?"

"He's a seventh grader. He's a bright little guy. I want him to come here."

"Should we get a bigger place?"

I could hear her sit up, see her silhouette move. She clicked on the lamp on your side of the bed. "I have to go home sooner or later."

I sat up too. "No. Tell him that I'm grieving and that I need a friend."

"That's not true, is it?"

"It's true. You know that I'm still in mourning. I am lonely too. You wouldn't be lying to him. Am I the first woman you've been with? I mean, is this the first time Jeffrey fought to bring you home?"

"No."

I sat back against the headboard and crossed my arms over my chest. I felt like a stupid girl. She asked me if I wanted a cigarette, and I couldn't answer. She said her son's name was Jeffrey Jr. and that he had ADHD and he drew pictures of naked women and penises all the time. "I don't mind because tits and ass keep him focused. And dick." She lit a cigarette, and I wanted her.

"Bring him here," I said.

"If I do that, he'd report me, Jeffrey Sr. He'd have both kids, and I'll be out on my ass. Well, I'll be here until you tire of me."

"I won't tire of you."

She looked at me with one eyebrow raised. She stared at me for a slow second, then shook her head. "It doesn't matter."

I lay back down and turned away from her. I felt anxious. My legs scissored back and forth. She put a hand on my back, and I stood and went to the bathroom. There I pissed, and then I paced the tile. I put on my robe and left the bathroom, my bedroom, down the hall to Shelly's. I knocked, and she didn't answer. I didn't know what time it was. I knocked again.

"Who—," I heard, the word disappearing into sleep.

"Shelly," I said.

"Yeah," she said.

"I'm coming in."

"Yeah."

Shelly was always a clean kid, and her room was as neat as a staged home on a realtor's showing. She lay like a vampire against her pillows, her arms and hands placed across her chest. I had a horrible thought that she, too, was dead and despaired because without her, I would have nothing. But she breathed, and I sighed away my irrational worry. I went to her and embraced her. I could feel her narrow chest beneath her nightgown, the skin, bones knitting themselves into adulthood. Was she still growing? Two years from now, she'd be gone. College or whatever. The thought made me hold her tighter. Because two years from now, I'd be alone.

"Mom," she said. She petted my head. "What is it? What time is it?"

"I don't have an answer for either one of those questions."

"You're too witty for the hour."

We quieted down, and Shelly held me in her arms. She fell back asleep, and I stayed there for a short while. I got up to leave, and she stopped me. "Eventually, she'll go home. Tonya says they always leave eventually."

"Yeah? Always, huh? Why does Tonya go along?"

"She's not too crazy about her father. Loves him, but she doesn't know what to do with him. And she feels like she has to watch her mother . . ."

"She told you this?"

". . . and wash the potatoes . . ."

"Go back to sleep, Shell."

Minnie has grown distant. She'd come home later at nights, and she didn't show up at rehearsals.

The play was going to premier in a week. Shelly and Tonya talked more, if only about the play, but Minnie and I talked less. I tried to busy myself with the play. I helped pass out flyers, and I assisted the costume designer with last-minute costume adjustments or changes.

On the first Thursday of December, the girls were at school, Minnie was at work, and I was home. Again, I started packing your things away for donation, and again, I must have stopped. I must have let my mind wander. I opened my eyes to find that my hands were shaking as they hovered over a box of windbreakers. I stood up, and it was too quick, the movement, and my head ached like I had fallen down on something solid. The doorbell rang.

Do you remember that I was the suicidal one and you were the happy one? My therapist (I had a therapist, and you did not. The weird thing, David, is that when you killed yourself, I stopped seeing my therapist. Just stopped going to her office. She knew. The whole town knew what happened. She came to the wake and told me, though I avoided her for most of the time that she was there and I would have gotten away with it if it were not for Shelly, that I ought to go see her. I only nodded at her. Then she called me that June, the first June, and I told her that I was in Mississippi because I was; Shelly and I were on that road trip) called my suicidal thoughts suicidal ideation. After a year of seeing her, she said that she believed that I would never hurt myself. I told you this. You nodded. I was the suicidal one! Now I can't imagine doing it. There was Shelly to consider.

I bent down again to take care of your windbreakers, but I couldn't get the box closed, or there was not enough in the box. I didn't know what the problem was.

Downstairs I heard Minnie talking to someone, their voices soft. I knew who it was. I listened as she walked up the stairs and came into the bedroom. Her face was drawn downward, and I could tell that she was older than me. "You're leaving," I said. She nodded.

"Does Tonya know?"

She nodded. "Jeff got her after school."

"Jeff. Was that him at the door?"

"Didn't you notice me packing?"

I had noticed her packing. Maybe that's why I tried packing your things again? I knew she was leaving. "What are you guys doing over Christmas break?" I asked.

She shrugged. "We usually go over into New Hampshire to visit Jeff's parents."

"Jeff. Do you love him, Minnie?"

"I love him enough. Are you going to be okay?"

"No. I will never be okay."

Minnie looked at me. She looked at the box and around the room. She knelt near me and slid the box away. "Don't do that yourself," she said. "Hire someone or have a friend come over and do it while you are away. Don't be here for that. Do you want me to do it? I can do that for you."

"You should go with Jeffry Sr."

"Do you want me to come out and get your husband's things?"

I stood up, and my head swam again. I faltered, and Minnie, standing up, reached out for me. "I don't want you to leave," I said, steadying myself in her arms. I tried not to cry, but I could feel myself crying. I refused to sob. "Just let go," I said. "Just leave."

She let go, and I stood up straight. She left the room, went down the stairs, left the house, and I left the room, I went down the stairs, left the house, left the door wide open. I walked after their car that Jeffry Sr. drove, my face immobile (I hoped), Minnie looking after me, looking at me with pity, and they picked up speed and drove away. I kept my pace, I kept walking.

You and I took this path many times, often after dinner on warmer days. Now it was nearly winter and cool, and I didn't have a jacket or sweater. I was just in a T-shirt. Maybe I was cool or even cold. Maybe I was still crying. I walked on into the woods on the little footpath, with the rickety wooden bridge that you swore beavers gnawed on, to the cackling creek that seemed to move slower in the heavy weather, to the little waterfall. I stood and watched the water, cloud white where it hit the rocks and window clear where it flowed in the creek. I stood there until I noticed the cold, and I stood there longer, and had Shelly not come, I would have stayed forever.

"So, Tonya and her mom are gone, huh?" she said.

I didn't answer. Shelly put her arm around me and pulled me in close to her. She had grown over an inch since you died. She was thin yet, but she was strong. She said, "I know you know this, but I miss him too."

"If you know I know this, then why say it?" She shrugged. I said, "What else is on your mind lately? It doesn't have to be about your father."

"There are a couple of things. A few things. Like, the play next week. I keep running through my lines. Paul Cormier, who is in the pit orchestra. He plays trumpet and trombone. I tried to introduce you to him at the party. I think we're dating? I'm thinking about why Dad did it. I'm worried about you, but you seem calm now. I mean, you're not doing anything but looking at the water."

"Calm?"

"What's on your mind?" she asked me.

"You are growing up, and I'm afraid that I'll miss something. Paul Cormier? I didn't know that. I'm missing things already. I'm distracted, I know. People are unhappy. Your father was unhappy. That sounds pat."

"It is pat."

"He loved us."

"That's pat too. Aren't you cold?"

"I'm cold, but we'll go home after I tell you this, okay? I didn't know Minnie's name until she came here for your party, but we used to talk during rehearsals. She'd go on and on about how great Tonya was. When she asked who was my child and I told her, she seemed wowed. You wow people, Shelly. You wowed your dad too. I don't want to be obvious, but I want you to know—"

"I know, Mom. People have depression."

"Okay. I also am thinking about what should I do next. I have to start working, right? Maybe? And next year is your last year of school. I don't want the same kind of job, though. I want something—oh, I was talking about you! This is all relevant."

"Mom, you're moving too fast again. Or you're talking too fast."

"I know. So, Minnie said that you were wonderful. She used the word *awesome*, and I guess since then, I've been going around looking at things and people in awe. Everyone and everything has something worthy of wonder and fear, of glory." I closed my eyes and tried to breathe in everything around me: the loamy dirt wet with melted snow and dead leaves, the crispness of the running water, the threat of a storm coming in from the northeast.

Trying to Balance

Beck bites my ear so hard my eyes tear. I pull away from him, and he pulls me closer. He has an erection. I move forward and try to focus on the macabre carnival animals going around the mirrored platform at a mesmerizing speed. One of us should be on the carousel, next to Bea, our daughter, helping her sit atop the flying horse.

The animals decelerate, and I look for Bea. I see her right before she rounds away out of sight, and I wave at her. She waves back. Then she is gone. The ride stops, and the people rush toward both the exit and the entrance. We go, too, to retrieve Bea, but she's not there. My heart thumps over the din of the carnival. There are too many people, too many kids Bea's size. Too many colors. We look through the crowd of summer clothing–clad kids and bare-legged adults moving away from the horses and dragons and flying beasts, looking for the wild tangle of Bea's hair.

"I don't see her," Beck says. He's on his tippy-toes, even though he's tall. I'm nearly kneeling, peeking through limbs, searching for my daughter. The carousel's animals start to fill up with new riders. Beck glares at me. He says, "I didn't want to pay for an extra ticket." He bends slightly away from me but jabs me with his elbow. It hurts enough to send me tottering. Then I realize that I'm afraid of two things: losing Bea and being with Beck.

"You stay here," he says. "I'll go around to the back of the merry-go-round. Okay?"

Instead of replying, I peer through the crowds and curse the descending sun. I look for Bea's amber curls catching beams of light in the whirls and kinks around her two Afro poofs. My love for her is singular. It is complete and free. My chest tightens at the thought of losing that kind of love. I think of those quiet moments only a few years ago when she was still nursing. She'd fall asleep with a mouth full of milk, and I would wipe her lips and cheeks clean, hoping not to wake her, wanting everything about that closeness we shared to last forever. "Bea," I cry out, more to myself, more to hear her name, not expecting a response.

But she answers. "Mommy."

And there she is: struggling, pulling away from a white woman with tree-trunk-thick legs. "Shut up," the woman says to Bea. "Stop it." The woman looks out of place. She's wearing a sweater though it's the height of summer. Her hair isn't combed, and her skin is unclean.

"Mommy!"

I run toward Bea. "That's my child."

"It is not," the woman says. "Clearly, it is with me. If it were yours, you would have kept a close watch on it. You would not have let it wander."

"Let go of my child!"

Beck hears me and comes running. An impromptu audience congregates around us, but none of its members come too close.

They silently watch, eating their cotton candy and sno-cones. The woman, Bea, Beck, and I are actors on an unapproachable stage. No one helps.

"Hey," Beck says. "Let go of my daughter."

"Well, which is it, huh? Is it yours," the woman points at me, "or yours?" She points at Beck. Neither of us seem to know how to react. We stay where we are but reach our hands toward our girl. Some in the crowd take video with their cell phones. Still, the horror show sound of the calliope music, the strained beating of my heart.

"Mommy," Bea yells, "Daddy, make her let me go. She is hurting me."

"Fuck it," the woman yells. "Fuck her. Get the fuck out of here." The woman pushes Bea toward us. Bea, crying, stumbles. I'm crying too. I grab at Bea, and Beck comes in. We hold her.

I lose sight of the woman; we all do. The spectators are all happy that we have Bea, but no one thinks to catch the woman or to call the cops.

We get on a packed shuttle bus. Some man is kind enough to offer his seat, so Beck sits down and puts Bea on his lap. It's so crowded that there are no free stirrups or poles to grab. "You'll have to surf, babe," Beck says.

I am trying to balance when the bus starts. Beck kicks my ankle with the tip of his boot. They are cowboy boots with silver tips. When he bought them, we were nearly broke and the rent was coming due. "I needed shoes," he told me then. I sold blood. And plasma.

He kicks me again. I look at him; he's looking out the window. My eyes sting, and someone behind me is touching my ass. I don't know if the touch is intentional or if it's because there is standing room only. The kick, the grope, they blend. I can't wait to get to our car. My father's old car. Daddy said it was too shitty for him to drive anymore. "But you need a car," he told me.

That night I hold Bea close to me before putting her into her canopy-covered princess bed. "I love you so much," then whisper, "please be gay."

"What does that mean?" she asks.

I bite my lip and consider my answer. "Be happy, Beatrice. Be happy."

Beck wakes me up with pinching my thighs with the nails on his right hand, the guitar picking hand where he let the fingernails grow long. I whimper. "Why are you doing this?"

"I don't know."

"Do you want to make love?"

"No."

I get up to get a glass of water. Later, in the kitchen, Beck comes behind me. He pulls my hair and yanks me back. The glass jerks forward and water falls from the rim, splashes across the kitchen. He was never abusive before, not so intentionally, but now this. I scream inwardly, not wanting to wake Bea. Beck pulls me all the way down to the floor, and the force hurts my neck, bangs my head against the tile. Little beads of light glitter before my eyes. He says, "I don't want to hurt you." He comes around from behind me and straddles me. He is naked except for his cowboy boots and eyeglasses.

The glass is still in my hand, and I stupidly wonder if there is still water in the glass. I am so thirsty.

"I am trying not to hurt you," he says.

This will certainly end, but I wonder how. Not wanting to stand anymore, I let myself sit in the shower, then lay as if bathing. What if Beck is out there, in the house? What if he comes in? I want to ask him what his long game is, but I don't know my own. We married because I missed a month, and instead of doing the responsible thing, we entertained the thought of what if. I'm not sure why we are still married. We are making the same mistakes countless couples have made before us.

I turn off the shower spray with my foot and let the hot water pour directly from the spout in a thick stream. Right onto my feet. I close my eyes and remember swimming under some nameless waterfall in northern Wisconsin. That was me in college before dropping out. I had taken women's studies classes, gone on road trips with girlfriends, and drunk beer straight from bottles in broad daylight.

I sit up and turn the water off. Outside, someone is beeping. I don't know it yet, but it's Beck; he's bought a beat-up pickup truck. And he's the one who will end it. He's the one who will say that it is unfair for me to be with him. "I don't know what I will do," he'll say to me. Maybe we won't be crying. Maybe we will. But he will look at Bea, and I will nudge him out the door.

Jubilee

Rosalie Shydale Lee kept her oldest daughter's hair cut short to less than an inch. She dressed her in baggy clothing. She kept her in on weeknights and most of the weekend. Rosalie sat on the bed with her daughter and prayed each night. Prayed and prayed against an unplanned grandchild, a failing grade, a molestation. Prayed for her husband to return, for the dog to stop shitting in the foyer, and for anything she could think of. And when she finished praying, she'd ask her oldest daughter, "Is there anything you want to ask of God?" to which her oldest daughter would answer, in her storybook princess way, "Only for your happiness, Mama."

"Oh, I am happy," Rosalie would say. "Spiritually, I am jubilant."

Rosalie Shydale Lee named her oldest daughter Florida. It was the state in which she conceived her child. Florida had never lived in Florida—a name she shared with an archetype from a 1970s television show, a name she refused to go by and preferred Lee. Lee, being a unisex name, often had people believe she was a boy when she was first introduced and often had other kids pick on her because of her forced androgyny. Years later, when her breasts would fill out her shirts and she'd wear her hair long and processed, she'd embrace the name Florida.

Florida Lee never told her mother, but she had met her real father when she was thirteen. She was still built like a boy, save for a slight curve in her buttocks, and her hair was still cut low. She had walked by him at the Juneteenth Day parade. He had excused himself after bumping into her in the crowd. He smiled at her, and it was so familiar that she stopped, her own smile caught like a lost word on her tongue. She had never reason to doubt that her mother's husband, who hadn't been home in almost three years, was her father, but when she saw that man smile, she knew that her life could have been something other.

He saw it too. He stopped and stared the girl up and down, his eyes not leering, just curious. Lee couldn't tell, at first, if it was lust or guilt she saw, but later she'd settle on curiosity. Remembering herself, she smiled at him.

"Baby girl," he said, the gap flashing at her from between his teeth just as in her smile. "You Rosalie's child?"

She nodded.

"Thought you were a boy with your hair cut in a fade like that."

"Mama keeps it short," she said.

"Tell her to let it grow," he said. *As if I hadn't considered that,* she thought. He reached into an inside pocket and pulled out a billfold. She noticed then how well he was dressed, how clean he was. "You take this, baby girl. You take care of yourself." He placed some bills into her hand. She folded them without looking at them. *Not until I get home,* she told herself.

She didn't pay attention to the rest of the parade. She didn't stay. She half-walked and half-skipped home, and when she got there—inside—she took out the bills and unfolded them. It felt like emancipation. Five one-hundred-dollar bills. Florida Lee didn't tell her mother she got them, and Florida Lee didn't know that this was not enough until years later, the years when she used the name Florida instead of Lee.

"Only for your happiness, Mama." Florida Lee bought a wig. It was a short wig, but it was feminine. She kept it in her book bag until she left the house and rounded the corner. She picked an alley with hardly any windows facing it. She donned the wig, using a little compact mirror so she could see to guide the wig on her head. Shiny wig full of sister locks. She looked good with hair. She got attention with hair. Other girls started talking to her, talking about her hair, talking about hair, asking her to do their hair, asking to do her hair.

The wig lasted for two months. Once, Rosalie waited for Lee in the alley. She was out of breath with running to catch the girl, to get there before her. "Why, baby?" she asked.

"I'm tired of looking like a boy."

"I only want what's best for you. Honey, I got pregnant with you when I wasn't even sixteen yet. I had to drop out of high school."

"You didn't have to."

"Don't talk back to me. Not in that voice. Not never. The things I did for you, Florida Lee, and what I continue to do."

And what you didn't do, Lee thought.

So back to short hair. Back to a high and tight. A fade.

Florida Lee went through puberty—despite her mother—when she was fifteen years old. Hair grew where Rosalie couldn't see to shave it, so Florida Lee shaved it herself. Her hips filled in, her butt popped so that men and boys noticed. Her stomach stayed flat. Her breast went from a double A to a B cup almost in a day. A month later she was in a C.

She began to spell her name *Leigh* on her school papers. The *i* dotted with a daisy. She wore large hoop earrings. Her short hair showed her long neck, how it proudly held up her brown head, how it stood erect between her broad shoulders. This emerging Florida Lee worried Rosalie.

In the mornings and when the girl got home from school and in the evenings, the two prayed—her mother listing endless needs and wants for herself, for Florida, for her other two children, for her husband to return.

Then Florida Lee wrote letters to her real father, whom she named Mr. Jackson Morehouse because it sounded powerful to her. Sometimes he was Mr. Booker King. Sometimes Muhammed X. Once she addressed the letter to Daddy.

Years later, when she would go by Florida, she would take her children camping, something she and her family had never done growing up. She would roast marshmallows and hot dogs with them. She would have a husband who had fathered all of her children, and he would be with them. They'd sing songs and tell horror stories. When it would be her turn to tell her story, she'd say, "I could tell you the story of my life, but I'm not sure if it's scary enough." Her life was the opposite of scary, she'd tell herself, a precautionary tale from day to day with misplaced hope. What does that happiness look like? That jubilee? And for all of her mother's so-called spirituality and for all of her prayer, she never took her children to church save for a funeral or a wedding.

And Florida Lee's hair would be long, black, and have an obsidian shine, catching the light from the moon; each star; and the campfire fueled by dried leaves and twigs, a log luckily found by her youngest son, and letters to a father she couldn't know.

The Claimer of Bodies

The Office of Decedent Affairs attendant removed some of the items Pearl had looked over. She came back with more files. Over one thousand bodies were represented in that room by scraps of paper, laminated identification cards, and postmortem photographs. Jewelry and hats. Grocery and to-do lists. Descriptions of the dead and nothing else.

The pictures were not the hardest thing to look at. In fact, Pearl looked at a photograph of a girl who kind of looked like Sandra. She was bothered how hard it was to tell whether it was Sandra or not. The problem was the skin. The skin looked paler than Sandra's, and Pearl considered the lighting in the examination room (or whatever room), the flash from the camera, the decay of the skin, the lighting in the room in which she now sat picking through the items from over a thousand dead people who were not claimed.

And this woman had extensions in her hair. Fat, two-strand twists listlessly fell from the woman's head. "Jane Doe" was written on the margin of the picture, along with "age: 20–35; race: Black or

Hispanic; name: unknown; height: 5'6"; weight at death: approx. 140 lbs."

"And you don't have any of the bodies?" Pearl asked.

"We cremate them all," the attendant said. She stood slightly behind and to the right of Pearl. She was a patient woman with brown, kind eyes. Pearl thought about how dismal this woman's job must be. The woman had spoken with a slight Central American accent, and Pearl couldn't imagine this woman coming all the way to the United States to dole out the remains of loved and unloved ones.

Pearl had told her that Sandra Jackson was her daughter, which was almost true. Sandra could have been her daughter, and in many ways she had helped raise Sandra. When she lived with Everette Jackson, who was Sandra's father, for those ten years, Pearl was entrusted with the shared task of disciplining and keeping the child. She fed her as if she were her own and bathed her when Sandra was still young. When Everette died, Sandra was kind enough to speak to Pearl at his funeral. And in the years since, they kind of kept in touch.

"How many women?" Pearl asked. "I mean, around Sandra Jackson's age?"

"There are only four we know who are exactly her age. Women that young are usually picked up by a family member. There are a couple of Jane Does whose ages are unknown."

"But all of her family is back in Wisconsin," Pearl said. She had flown to California the day before to look for Sandra. She had read that the previous year's unclaimed dead were to be buried in December. The last she heard from Sandra, the area code was from California. "This is the last time, Mama Pearl," Sandra had said. Pearl always hated and loved being called Mama Pearl, by Sandra or by anyone. It showed that she was loved and that she didn't have any children of her own. Her own child, Pearl knew, would have just called her Mama.

"How much you need this time?" Pearl had asked Sandra. That was nearly a year ago.

"Just two hundred and forty," she had said. "It's for rent at this place I'm staying. Mama Pearl, I don't want to be on the street."

"Where are you staying?" Sandra had said she was in Los Angeles chasing a dream. And Pearl hadn't heard from her since. Many nights she had wondered if the girl had found her way, or maybe she had moved to some other city or state. Out of all people, Pearl was disappointed in Sandra. The girl had a future, but she threw it away.

"How many of these are babies?" Sandra asked, not wanting to ask. What came to mind unexpectedly were tossed babies and back-alley aborted fetuses.

"I didn't give you any of the babies," the woman said.

"I know, but how many?"

"One hundred and thirty-one."

"How did they die?"

"All different ways."

"In hospitals ever?"

"In hospitals."

Pearl cleared her throat. The sound was ugly and loud. It echoed off the walls. The woman moved forward. She had a name and title: Officer Carillo or Castizo. She now put her hand on Pearl's shoulder, still slightly behind her, still to her right. "Are you okay?" the woman asked.

Pearl nodded. She picked up another folder. Inside there were two photographs in front. The first was of a tattoo that read "Pug Life." A badly rendered picture of a dog was inked in beneath it. The second was a picture of an ear with piercing holes up and down the lobe and one on the tragus. A mark of keloid was noticeable behind the meaty part of the person's lobe. The skin was too dark. This was not Sandra. Besides, Pearl was sure that Sandra had no tattoos. From what she knew of the girl, she was bothered immensely by needles.

Could Pearl take home some Jane Doe's ashes and give them a proper disposal, then get a surprise call from Sandra later asking for money? Pearl closed the folder and set it aside off to her right. She picked up another folder and opened it to a woman whose eyes and lips were sewn shut. Her nose was plugged with cotton. She had a pink scar beneath her eye. This woman was white.

"Sorry," Officer Carillo or Castizo moved in quickly and took away the two folders, both Pug Life and scarred white woman.

"How many have I looked through?"

"About fifty."

"Hundreds more," Pearl said. She shook her head. She didn't even know if Sandra was dead. But wouldn't it kill her, Pearl thought, if she did not go and try to discover Sandra in the files of Los Angeles's unclaimed? If Sandra's mother wasn't too strung out on whatever the now-popular drug—meth or heroin—Pearl would have contacted her to go instead or inquire after her child. But since there was no one, and since Pearl had nothing else to do, and since Pearl didn't want another person to be left to an unceremonious mass grave—not another one whom she could help—Pearl took it upon herself to buy a ticket to LA and look for Sandra.

"When you bury these people," Pearl asked the attendant, "will there be a ceremony?"

"They don't each get their own grave, if that's what you're asking. There will be a mass grave. There is a ceremony." Pearl tried to picture it. Maybe a prayer would be read where county workers would bow their heads and try to feel something for ignored and forgotten ashes in plain boxes.

"Sometimes," the lady said, "it saddens me that so many of these people, children especially, are left to eternity without a loved one to say goodbye."

Sometimes, Pearl thought. This was the worst job, she was sure, the gatekeeper of the lost, the forgotten, the unloved. Pearl picked up a box in which an expensive watch sat on top of a picture of a tattoo. The tattoo read "Roger: RIP July 1, 1984 to July 2, 2013." The dead honoring the dead. Pearl looked at the watch again. If she were to start claiming strangers, she'd be smart to start with this one, but she wasn't interested in her (age: 20–35; race: Black) or the watch. She wasn't interested in the next one either. There was a picture of the woman, dead and sewn up (her skin too brightly peachy tan to be Sandra's), and another picture, probably found in the woman's purse. Smiling next to a man with a goatee and Afro. Both stood proudly in front of an orange pickup truck. No.

Pearl wanted to demand to see the babies. She thought about telling the attendant, "I know a lost baby," but how would she explain that knowledge? She'd have to be the mother or someone close.

Years ago she was the mother or someone close. She had held her baby, who had lived for nearly an hour. "Twenty-three years ago," she said aloud but so quietly that the attendant could not have understood her even if she had heard.

Her baby was blue. Unnamed, bluish-black ugly thing in an industrially knitted cap and a hospital onesie. Diapered. Head still smooshed from passing through the birth canal. Pearl could not handle it. She was left alone to say goodbye to her daughter. She placed the baby on the bed and kissed her head. Stiff and cooling. "You are Myneisha," she said. All her hopes and dreams for still making it through high school and later college, even with a baby, disappeared. But she felt lightened. Relief. "You are Myneisha," she repeated as she got dressed, "and I would have loved you."

When she checked in that day, she had told the hospital that her name was Thelma Warner. She had lied about her phone number, her address, her next of kin. No one in her life knew she was pregnant. She wasn't even sure—too scared to go and get tested. And now no one would ever know. Pearl had thought then that on her worst days, she would remember Myneisha, but she remembered her every day. She thought about her and her big brown eyes flat as a photograph not staring back at her. It was too much. She could not handle it. Who could blame her?

"This one," she said. "I know this one." She held up a picture of a young woman whose skin was caramel colored and whose hair was matted with blood. Her eyes looked sad, even though they were closed. "I will claim her."

"Is that," the attendant asked, reading the paper in her hand, "Sandra Jackson?"

"No, but I know her." Pearl picked up another folder and looked inside. An obese, dark-skinned woman with dreadlocks stared dumbly back at the camera. "Her too."

"You know that this costs money. You will be charged the cost for cremation for both of those women."

"This young woman," Pearl said, picking up another folder at random and not even looking inside, "is a good friend of my family. And this one," another picture, "married my second cousin."

"I want to do the same thing," the woman said. She moved forward and bent down on her haunches. "I want them all to have love or to be cared about, but it can't happen."

"I know these women," Pearl said. "I know them all." Sandra Jackson was not there among the hundreds of dead women, but she might as well have been, as far as Pearl was concerned. "These women are good enough."

The attendant, not Pearl, cried. "They are all good enough," she said.

"So, I will claim them. I will claim these four women." Pearl picked up another folder. "These four women will go home, and each will get her own place."

The attendant wiped her face with the back of a hand. "Holy Hannah," she said. "Okay. It's not the first time someone has done something like this. But I can't let you take them."

"Then give me someone. Give me the Jane Does."

The attendant turned away and came back with two, slim boxes. She handed them to Pearl. "Please, keep this to yourself."

Sandra Jackson kept checking her watch. She kept rocking back and forth in her seat. She looked too skinny. "Are you warm enough?" Pearl asked. It was a stupid question. They were eating alfresco at a little café on Venice Beach. It was hot that day.

"I am. Just anxious. I was surprised to hear from you." She took a sip of water. Pearl had tried the number Sandra had called from earlier that year. She should have called before hopping on a plane to look for her body. But maybe she needed the trip. Maybe she needed to spend some money. What was she doing with it anyway?

"It's good to see you. I want you to know that you can call anytime still. I know your father's been gone for a while, but I will always be there for you."

"What's in these boxes."

"Hmm?"

"These boxes." The two boxes of ashes rested atop the dining table. Sandra tapped on the top one. "Are these presents for me?"

"I don't have presents for you. I mean, I have this lunch for you that I'm buying. I can give you money."

"Really, Mama Pearl, I don't need money. I want to hold onto what I said last we talked. It was the last time."

"You've said that before."

"Yeah, but this time I mean it. I've had a few acting gigs. And I think I got on a reality show."

"You can call even if you don't want money."

"Why are you in LA?"

"For these boxes."

"And what's in these boxes?"

Pearl smiled. Instead of answering, she asked Sandra questions. She wanted to hear more about the girl's life and how she was pulling her way out of drugs and into the life of a starlet. "It's anonymous, right? But I'm in Narc Anon." She nodded her head and listened to Sandra. She ate her food when it came and wondered, absently, how she will give the women beside her a proper burial or whatever it is she will do with the ashes. She closed her eyes briefly and imagined shaking the women free when she returned home. She saw their ashes catch the welcoming wind.

Your Father Died

Your father died, and everyone feels stupid about it. Your mother is inconsolable, half-sitting and half-laying on the overstuffed ottoman that your father liked to rest his feet on. In the house everything looks like him. You can smell him: his brand of cigarettes that he smoked in stages (three puffs and stub out; four puffs and stub out; lights, then hits; then lets burn), his cologne he wore for years, his hair gel. He was the kind of man who wore hair gel to both darken his hair and tame it. He was the kind of man whose hair was curly, but he hid it. You look around the house, and you cannot not see him. He's everywhere.

Your mother is crying still. She's been crying since you got there. Her sobs are now hoarse, and somehow that makes them more pitiful. You can't see if there are tears because her face is placed down on the ottoman, away from you. She won't talk to you. She won't talk to nobody. You can hear her correcting your English in your head. "Anybody," she would say were she not crying, worried that people would blame your bad English on her African American and your father's Puerto Rican background. Appearances, your mother. She was always about appearance, except for now because she is crying regardless of the well-wishers and consolers who came and went, bringing casseroles and dessert bars and bottles of name-brand colas.

So much food. And flowers. Flowers overflowed on tabletops, chairs, and counter space. The three bookcases were covered with vases of lilies and roses, daffodils and tulips. "Of course she's so broken," you hear one of the people around your parents' age say from the kitchen, "he was so young." You walk toward the kitchen and sneak a peek to see the woman who knew a thing about premature deaths. She is your parents' age, you're sure. Face pasty and beginning to wrinkle. Late sixties or early seventies. You think something silly but seemingly witty: age is relative, especially in matters of love and death. It's an embarrassing thought, so you don't say it. You only give the woman a terse smile. You can't cry.

Your father died, and you can't cry. He loved you. Doted on you! Bought you toys and candy without prompting. He picked you up in his arms and danced you around, singing in Spanish songs of lament. You loved him! You would grab his jowls, squeeze his cratered face, and squeal. It was an important father-daughter love. You smiled more when thinking about it. He died, and you smiled at some strange woman, dumbly thinking in the back of the mind that maybe he wasn't a saint, maybe he took this woman, this thinning blonde with thinning hair, and pushed her greedily against the wall. Maybe he let his large, working hands work his way up her nyloned thighs. Maybe he nibbled her neck when your mother was in the kitchen cooking the main course, stirring something, getting more hors d'oeuvres. You kind of hoped he did.

Or maybe not. Not your father. You just wanted to feel angry. You just wanted to feel okay about his dying. "He was young," you say. "But still, he lived a good life."

Part II

Your brother Gustavo, the youngest, is in the house again. He says your name. You don't know what he wants. You turn to him, and he hugs you, and it hurts to hug him in a way that it hurts to pick up a bag of hard food, like uncooked potatoes or early apples or pineapples, and you hug him back, but you want to let him go. Gustavo is hot from the sun outside, where he and Natalia and Renee and Emmanuel and Roberto are, trying to stay away from relatives and well-wishers. You gently push Gustavo away.

"What is it?" you say.

"Let's get Mama some rum and cola, huh? That's what she wants. Spiced rum."

"You and me?"

"All of us."

You look outside, and you see all of your sisters and your other brothers—Natalia, Renee, Emmanuel, and Roberto—in Emmanuel's cargo van. Who drives a cargo van anymore? A man who will allow no shortened version of his name, that's who. Your dad has died, and all of your brothers and sisters are in a van, looking at you and your little brother. And you can't cry. You don't cry, but you laugh because your mother, in her pain, is now only moaning a low growl behind you.

Rum and beans and rice, you say. But you're not sure if Gustavo is listening. He walks outside toward the rest of the family, and you think about the hubris to believe death could ever be premature.

PART III

It is connected in my mind . . .
with a very odd story.

—ROBERT LOUIS STEVENSON,
The Strange Case of Dr. Jekyll and Mr. Hyde

A black cat comes, wide-eyed and thin;
And we take him in.

—THOMAS HARDY,
"Snow in the Suburbs"

Tiger-Free Days

The telephone poles looked like crucifixes. I had the time to contemplate them, and that was how silent it was. We all remained inside like the person on the radio demanded us to. We looked out the large window, having pushed aside displays of shelved books and tea sets to see the large, male tiger, his testicles hanging noticeably from his crotch. From inside, we could hear the half-growling, half-purring noise he made. We probably more felt it than heard it. It was low. He paced.

"How long will he stay out there?" someone behind me said. I recognized the voice, but I had a hard time placing a disembodied voice to the person. I always had. I had a hard time understanding what was said without looking at the person who spoke. "Why hasn't," a woman asked, "anyone come to get him yet?" I went through the schedule in my head and remembered that Julie was the only other woman besides me working the floor that day. What I could think of to answer was that not all our days can be tiger free. After I had said it, I backed away from the window. Someone arrived in an armored car marked "zoo." And also: some cop cars. An animal control van. I could hear the report from the tranquilizer gun. I thought of those savior-less telephone poles, the wires going to everywhere.

Ballad of Jane

Jane's shoes were too tight. She smiled at her date, Edgar, who thought he knew everything and aimed to tell her everything. They sat across from each other at a little bar table, on little bar chairs with bent cast-iron backs, fashioned into crossing hearts. "That's how they make wine forgoing the oak—it creates a fresher flavor," he said. She smiled, she nodded, she let her shoes slip off her heels, she felt the flesh pulse out there. She'd need moleskin. "Some go in for that, but I like that muted, woody taste. More Old World, ain't it?" he asked. He spoke with too much breath. She nodded.

"You like wine? What's that you drinking? Very sweet, ain't it?"

"I like my wine dry," she said. "It's a Malbec. Australia, of course."

"Of course. Dry wine. I've figured you wetter."

What? "What did you—"

"Your taste in wine."

"It's dry." Her feet were killing her. Jane turned away from him. She looked toward the bar. What were they doing at a bar?

"Did you like the movie?" Edgar asked. What grown man took his date to a movie? She shrugged. "How long did you say you've been divorced?"

She sighed. She wanted to leave. She turned back toward Edgar. "A little over a year. Thirty-four days over a year. Three hundred ninety-nine days. And each of those days, I count as a blessing. *Blessing*'s not the right word. Whatever the word for it, I'm happy for them."

"Irreconcilable differences?"

"You could call Amanda Jackson irreconcilable. I don't want to talk about that. Let's talk about something else. You've never been married, so let's not talk about that or why."

"You want to get out of here?"

"With you?"

He grinned at her with one eyebrow raised. "Has it been four hundred days?"

She grinned back. "More than that."

Jane felt too old for regrets. Edgar slept beside her with some contraption on his face, strapped around the back of his head, affixed to his nose and mouth. His chest sunk in, curly graying hairs concaved in denser darkness. And his belly was convex. Also hairy. She reached over him in his single bed and grabbed his pack of cigarettes. Menthol. She hadn't smoked in over fifteen years, and she never smoked menthol. Yet she shook one out and found his lighter. She lit it and inhaled and exhaled quickly. Like riding a bike. She inhaled and took it in. Her head ballooned. Exhaled.

Scott, her son, probably wondered where she was, but Scott didn't care. Who could blame him? He was fifteen and knew everything. Her ex-husband knew everything too. She should get home to him, though. To Scott. Before the sun rose. She took in a few more drags of the cigarette, then reached across Edgar and put it out in his ashtray.

"I will have to put those shoes back on," she said.

In the parking lot of her apartment complex, Jane saw a squirrel and blue jay squaring off. Such a small plot of dirt. Spring mud, really. Little sprouts of grass, some yellowed grass, squirrel, bird, maybe a buried nut. The squirrel chattered as she knew squirrels do. The jay, too, made a noise. A high-pitched screech. It was unnerving.

At home Scott was not sleeping. He was up playing video games online with millions of people he'd never know. The two, mother and son, grunted at each other. "You smell like a brewery," he said.

"You talk in clichés," she said. "Did you eat anything?"

"I ordered a pizza."

"You used my credit card?"

"I don't have one of my own."

"I don't know how much I owe on that thing, Scott."

"I didn't leave my son at home with nothing to eat."

"You could have called your dad." She had already taken her shoes off. She had already put her purse away and removed her pantyhose. She now stepped behind her son and petted his head.

"I hate that, Mom."

"I know." She continued to pet his head. "Is this all you did today?"

"And homework."

Later she'll sleep in her own bed, queen sized, which she had shared with her ex-husband. Four hundred days ago.

"If you get all As, we'll go to Disneyland."

"I'm too old for that. I'll go. How would you pay for it?"

"Child support."

They ate cold cereal at the kitchen table. She closed her eyes and saw her bungalow only four blocks from the lake, with the long front yard and the big backyard. She saw her garden of wildflowers in front, the vegetables she grew out back, the apple tree, the pear tree. She opened her eyes, and it was all gone. "If you get As and Bs, we'll go camping."

"Can I bring a friend?"

"You can bring a friend camping, yes. You think you're going camping, huh?"

"Ain't no way I'm getting all As."

She closed her eyes again and imagined her backyard. She grew peas there and snap beans. She grew tomatoes, cucumbers, squash, and peppers. Once she had found a deer in her yard, munching on peas.

"Can I bring a girlfriend?"

"Of course not," she said, eyes still closed.

Jane walked along the lake with a man called Bobby, but she wasn't sure of his first name. His profile said it was Jonathan. His last name was listed as Piotrowski. She asked him about it, and he said that his grandfather said he looked like a Bobby. "He said, pointing at me with his bent index finger, 'You are so fat, you should be called Bobby.'" They both laughed.

"He didn't say you look like a Bobby. He said you were fat. Oh, my God, you were fat?"

"I was. I was a 120-pound eight-year-old. All of four feet or so too."

"I can't see it. You're so, you know, fit."

"Yeah, well, back then I ate and ate, and you know, Jane, I just sat. Cheese Puffs, Oreos, and video games. And traditional foods too—I ate pierogi by the handful."

Jane laughed again. "You look great now."

"Thanks. You're not too bad yourself, of course."

Jane said, "So, my lunch hour's almost over. You think you want to do this? See each other for a date?"

"A real date?" He nodded his head. "This was nice."

"But let's not go to a movie," she said.

Scott was petting some woman's dog. Jane thought the woman was Amanda Jackson, but it was just another young woman with brick-red hair and a round behind. "Hi," Jane said.

"Hello," the woman said. There was a long *w* at the end of that word. "You want to pet the dog too?"

"No," Jane said. "This is my son."

The dog looked up at Jane. He looked confused. Its face and muzzle were surrounded by fur that radiated out like a lion's mane. "It's a chow," Scott said. It was full of fur.

"They fight in China," the woman said. "Chow or chow chow. He's my little Ookie Bear. That's his name."

"Come on, Scott. Let's go home."

"Excuse my mother. She only likes petting me."

Scott was always on something electronic. Mostly, he was plugged into his phone, talking or listening to music. Even when he was playing games, he'd have his earphones on. They were retro-bulky and swallowed even his large ears. In this way the little apartment they shared became silent. The tinny noise from Scott's phones, the steady breathing from Jane. Eventually, she began speaking aloud to herself. Little words at first. *Huh, see, funny, where, shit.* She spoke while doing things like reading or cooking. Then the single words grew to sentences. To conversations. Reading aloud was enjoyable.

Scott found her having a complete conversation: "Is that so? Looked like Amanda. In a way every woman I know looks like Amanda." She laughed. "I'm so fucked-up. He's so over me. Why am

I still thinking about them? Is he even with Amanda anymore? But you, Bobby's nice. Fourth date since the divorce, first with Bobby. I don't even know what to do on a date."

She felt watched and looked up to see her son staring at her. Obviously, he was worried about her.

Jane wore comfortable shoes. They stayed tied securely to her feet as she ate her lobster roll. Across from her, Bobby told her a story about camping. He had encountered a frog on that trip. "A rabid frog," he said.

"Frogs don't get rabies," she said.

"I know! But this frog, maybe he was on something. Maybe he licked himself!"

Jane giggled.

"You know frogs are supposed to run away, right?"

"You can hardly find them when you're looking," Jane said. "All croaks until you get near them."

"Right! But this frog, he came after me."

She giggled again and took another sip of her beer. "Too much of this, and I won't be any good shooting a paint gun."

"You'll be fine. You know, I ran from that frog?"

Scott had gotten three As, two Bs, and a B-minus. "I don't know if we'll camp with a minus on the card."

"That's not fair, Mom. You said nothing about the quality of the grade."

"'The quality of the grade'? Is that what we call plus and minuses now? Calm down. We'll go camping. Who are you taking with you?"

"Oakland."

"Oh, great. The kid named after a city."

"That's not his real name. His real name is Del something. Delany maybe?"

"Maybe I prefer Oakland. He can come along."

"I'll go call him," Scott said.

Jane was left alone at the kitchen–dining room table. She looked over Scott's report card and was glad that her son was doing pretty well, much better than she did when she was fifteen. "I'll have to call his father," she said, and thinking it and saying it made her chest hurt. "But I had a good time with Bobby." Welts from the paint gun hits were still on her skin in three places. She liked the pain and marks from the pellets. She considered them evidence of a good time. Jane stood up and retrieved the cordless phone and sat down again. Her thumb rubbed the rubber keys lightly. She hated calling her ex-husband, even for little things like sharing her son's grades. But it was not exactly little; she would have to ask for money, too, for their camping trip. She assured herself that it was her right to the money, and he owed it to Scott too. She dialed home. Her husband answered. "Jane," he said. "What is it?"

"Hi, Christopher. How are you?"

"The sky is blue, and the sun's bright."

"It is."

Tears that felt both fake and overly real fell. She didn't sob. "Scott's got his report card today. B-minus in government. Otherwise, all As and Bs. He got an A-plus in pre-calc."

"Impressive kid."

"We should be proud." She wiped her nose with the back of her hand. "I can't see how you can still stay in that house. Of course, it's I who was hurt there, not you."

"Is there anything else, Jane?"

"I want to take him camping."

"You need some money."

"And you're behind on child support. You should get him a present too. I mean, he's doing so well in math, and he's not even a senior yet. I'll send Scott. Put it in an envelope."

When she hung up, she let out a deep sob that involved her entire throat. Scott was in the kitchen again, perusing the contents of the cabinets, but he couldn't possibly hear her with his earphones on.

There was a feral cat on the hood of the car. In the back seat, Scott sat with his friend Oakland, both plugged into their cell phones via headphones, both texting furiously. They couldn't hear Jane's command for them to get the cat off the car, so she had to take care of it herself. She shooed it with her hands, said, "Scat, cat, we've got to go." She wanted to get there before four, but they'd have to leave immediately. She reached toward the cat, and its fur fluffed out, visually expanding its size. It hissed, drawing its non-lips back from its teeth. Its eyes glowed.

"Whoa," Jane said. And the cat hissed again. Made a mad growl deep in its guts. "Fuck," Jane said. She backed up and looked for something. She didn't want to hurt it, only to scare it. She couldn't blame it: it was a cold morning. It was still spring. The car hood was warm, and the car was still. The car was his, as far as the cat was concerned. "Okay, cat, you're going to have to go."

She closed her eyes and saw her two-car garage just four blocks from the lake. "Fuck. What can I use here?" Inside, her ex-husband ("call him Christopher, damn it") had nailed hooks onto the walls. On them were the outside tools: rakes and shovels and brooms and ice scrapers. Here there was nothing because it was an apartment complex. What does a tenant need with a shovel? A rake? "Four fucking blocks from Lake Drive!" she said. The cat growled again, a menacing purr.

"You need help with the cat, Mrs. Silver?"

"Ms. Silver. Sure, Oakland. You can call me Jane."

Oakland took his chained wallet from his pocket. He swung it around, moving it above his head like a lasso. The cat followed the movement of the wallet with its face. It sat up on the hood of the car, its little face circling slightly along with the wallet.

"Don't hurt him."

"I won't." Quickly, Oakland let the wallet drop near the cat. The chain made a shimmery noise. The cat snarled and jumped back, then down. It ran away, all claws out, still extra-fluffy.

"Thank you, Oakland."

"No problem," he said. He went back into the car, the back seat. Jane breathed in deeply and joined the boys in the car, taking the wheel. Her lower back hurt, and her stomach felt tight. "Shit," she said. She left the car and ran back to the house for tampons. Then she ran back to the car and climbed in behind the wheel. "Superior, here we come."

By three o'clock they were nearing their campsite. "We are making awesome time," Jane said to herself. Scott and Oakland were both asleep. By four o'clock Jane was showing Oakland how to tie a fly on his rod. Scott had tried to show his friend, but he gave up in a fit of giggles.

"It's not that hard," Jane told Oakland. "Look, don't overthink it. First, take the backing and wrap it around the backing tool."

"The backing tool?" Scott said.

"Wrap the backing about six or eight times around the tool here. This is a nail knot."

"The tool?" Oakland asked.

"No, the kind of . . . just wrap it around." Eventually, everyone's line was ready, and the trio fished. Their lines arced expertly across the sky, especially Jane's, and everyone caught something. Oakland's fish, a huge rainbow trout that was at least twenty-two inches long, was the biggest. They went back to camp and fried their fish up. They all three talked and laughed over dinner, then Scott and Oakland plugged themselves back in.

Before the sun went down entirely, Jane wanted to go for a walk. She grabbed her flashlight and waved at the boys until they noticed her, until they noticed that she was going away. She wasn't afraid of being alone. Actually, Jane felt rather at home camping. These woods she had visited many times with her father and with her own family when she was still with Christopher. Because she had known these grounds before Chris, she didn't feel that it was something she couldn't revisit. It wasn't the home they bought together; it wasn't their life they built together; it was these trees and waters that were here ages before her and would be here long after she was gone. Her life mattered little here. She found this comforting.

Jane spied a neat little spot leaning downhill. She took down her pants to relieve herself. When she wiped, she was disappointed to see that she was on her period for sure. She believed blood attracted creatures, and the wrong type of creatures. She finished up and wiped her hands on the leaves around her. She continued to walk.

There was still plenty of light. The smell of the woods this time of year, between late spring and early summer, was loamy. Earthy. But there was the clean smell of running water, too, just thawed and cool. This far up north, between Wisconsin and Minnesota, the waters weren't quite thawed all the way for the year because it was still pretty cold. Sometimes you can see snow pockets, even this late in the season.

There was something moving. With her? Near her? "Scott?" If it were Scott, he didn't answer. And this moving thing's tread was heavy. Even but too quick for two feet. Jane heard steps like one, two, threefour; one, two, threefour. Her heart felt too big and too loud. Shh shh, she said to her heart. The blood coursing through her head. Shh shh. She stopped moving.

It stopped moving.

Quietly, quickly, Jane looked around. Up, down, everywhere. The leaves seemed too concealing, too conspiratorial. Why would they reveal one of their own, a creature of these woods? Jane was just a visitor who tramped around their grounds and stole their fish.

It moved again. One, two, threefour. Jane's teeth chattered involuntarily, and she ended that. She clamped her mouth shut. It was still moving. Away? Nearer? Oh, fuck, was she talking aloud? She was. She turned and saw what she knew would be there. A bear. It was not fully grown, but it was no cub. It was a juvenile black bear. It was probably about 200, 250 pounds, which was at least 100 pounds more than Jane. It had probably just been booted from the comfort of home by its mother because it was old enough to fend for itself. And it was very obviously an unhappy and hungry young bear. Its nostrils flared, and it breathed in, breathed her in. Its ears were large and, more than likely, listening to her constant chatter.

It growled, its lips vibrating and showing her its gums and a flash of its teeth. It smelled her blood, she knew, and it heard her clumping through the forest and talking to herself. It roared. The force of it made her nearly empty bladder release more urine. Just more scent for him to mark her by. She thought about her situation and remembered advice. She lifted her body high, hands into claws, and screamed. It backed away a little, confused, but it came back, raising its black, shiny body on its hind paws and raised its own arms above its head. Roared.

Jane was no good. She cried now, sobbed. Her nose ran, and she instinctively sniffled. The bear would not shut up. Its fury reduced her, shook her, and shamed her. Finally, it grabbed Jane and violently shook her. She cried, calling her son's name, calling her husband's name, calling the name of every man she ever knew. Her father's son, whose name was Jessie, over and over, until it turned into *Jesus*.

The bear didn't care. It shook her and roared into her face.

She pushed against the beast, blathering still. It took a stronger hold of her, wrapping its arms about her. She heard something snap and felt a pang in her right shoulder that brought little dancing rays of shooting light to her eyes. "Please," she said. This was now her mantra, having left off from *Jesus*. The bear didn't know *Please* any more than it knew *Jesus*. It squeezed more. It had stopped roaring and now just kind of groaned into her face, her neck.

This could be nice, Jane thought, if it weren't so violent. She let her body slacken, and the bear loosened up. Maybe it was just toying with her, and maybe now it was tiring out. Maybe now it'll let her free. Jane tried pulling away, but the pain in her shoulder caught her, made her scream anew. The bear roared again and then snorted. It tightened its grip. Jane didn't react this time. She closed her eyes and remembered her mother comforting her after school or embracing her to brace her for something painful, like a vaccination shot. She imagined her ex-husband, pre–Amanda Jackson, holding her. She wrapped her arms around the bear and leaned in. This, too, confused the bear, and it relaxed a bit. But its primal needs reminded it why it was there, and it squeezed. Jane squeezed too. "Christopher."

The bear, not Christopher, pushed into Jane now with its paws, letting its claws dig into the flesh of her arm. She felt the hot blood make its way down her forearm, her hand. That frightened her, got her. She went limp with fear.

She was going to die.

The bear, reacting to Jane's weight shifting, embraced her tighter to hold her up. Its wet nose and fuzzy face were against her face, her jaw, her neck. What could be kinder, Jane thought, than a hug before dying?

Free Fish

We sampled the sushi though it was suspect. What did white people know about sushi? "What white people don't know?" Adam asked.

"They know every fucking thing if you give them a minute," I said.

"We'll feel this later. We'll have sour stomachs, and we'll retrace everything we ate."

"Then one of us would remember the white people sushi." We were aware that the vendors could hear us, but we didn't care. They pretended that they couldn't hear us. We bought two fish. I don't even remember what kind. And we bought fresh sea salt in a clay pot. Adam asked, "Can salt really be fresh?" and the vendors gave him an answer that I can't remember.

Halfway through our excursion at the farmers market, we realized that there was so much fish and seafood because we were on the coast, in the Cape. "It makes perfect sense," Adam said. "Why didn't that dawn on us before?"

I didn't answer. We walked around and bought last fall's apples and New England donuts. Then we took our packages of fish, apples, and donuts and sat on one of the many piers on the bay. We ate apples after rubbing them on our shirts. Then we ate donuts. "We can't take fish back to the hotel room," I said.

"Maybe they'll fry it up for us."

"Who? This ain't the Caribbean."

Adam shrugged. "Should we set them free?"

"Free? Adam, honey, these fish have been dead for a long time."

"How long?" He took the fish and unwrapped them carefully. The creature on his lap lay lifeless. Its opened, unseeing eye stared out. The other eye lay against Adam's leg. A whole life in profile. "You want to touch them?"

"I've touched fish before."

I watched as Adam rubbed a finger the wrong way across one of the fish's scales. "I don't know fuck one about fish."

"Me neither," I said. "Why don't we set them free."

"When do you think they were caught?"

I shrugged. "Adam, I want to kiss you."

Adam shook his head no. We were in an uncomfortable spot. I made it that way. But we had tickets to Massachusetts and plans, so we kept them. "I'm still in love with you," I said.

He dumped the fish in the ocean without ceremony and without another word. I was tired of apologizing, so I didn't. We watched the fish float on the little ripple waves there on the coast. And later we'll watch horrible television that is mostly flipping through channels, not knowing the schedule in a strange town. We will each sleep awkwardly on separate hotel beds. And tomorrow? What will we do tomorrow?

The fish floated a little farther away from us. Their glassy eyes looked upward at everything. Their silver-scaled bodies reflecting the sun just like the waters around them.

Cat, Catfish, Cat

for Helen Lampkin

I. CAT

What does one do with her hair for a date of catfishing in the Untethered Lagoon? These were the days before the proper ponytail and permanent, and pomade would sweat and drip. What Jo-Alice did was take her hair, straightened by a hot iron comb with thinly spaced teeny teeth, and put it into four big braids. She then took a kerchief and wrapped that around her head. And what does one wear? Saddle shoes, socks over her stockings, and a dark dress that won't stain. That is what Jo-Alice wore.

Charles, she saw, had more freedom. He wore denim overalls and a clean shirt. His hair was cut low and pomaded. Little rose-shaped curls grew all over his head. He carried a tackle box. She carried a picnic basket. They met right at Jo-Alice's gate, before the sun rose, before the first roosters woke to wake everyone else. "Can you see me, Charles? It's so dark out yet."

"I can see the shape of you," he said. "And I can sense your beauty. Girl, I can smell it."

"You're smelling the cold chicken I got packed here in this basket."

"I have two fishing poles," Charles said. "I'm going to teach you to fish." His *going* sounded like *gone*.

"Who say I don't know how?" Jo-Alice asked.

The two walked beside each other, slowly, hardly talking. They listened to the day begin with the buzzing of cicadas and the dying out of the cricket song. "Going to be hot today," she said, and her accent was just like his. "This may be the last thing I do today, fishing with you."

"Then it'll be a good day. We'll catch some big muddy monsters. Your mama could fry them up for y'all. She make good catfish?"

"What a rude question, Charles. I wonder about your upbringing sometimes. What you think?"

They came to a walking bridge that didn't have a name, but it was the bridge that brought everyone to Untethered and away again. You could only walk from this point: no horses, no cars. The bridge could fit three abreast but not very comfortably. Two side by side was perfect, but with their basket and tackle box, Jo-Alice and Charles walked pretty close together. It was a rope bridge with wooden planks. No one knew who built it, but everyone assumed it was slave work long ago, the days before pressing combs and the carelessness of early-morning fishing.

"You are getting too close, Charles," Jo-Alice said. She considered herself a forward-thinking woman, but Charles was acting too sure of himself.

"It's a narrow bridge."

"Narrow, my ass."

"It is. We got to let that cat pass."

"That what?"

"Up yonder. Look."

Jo-Alice saw the glow of the animal's eyes before she saw the actual animal. Two gold-green globes of light that now narrowed at her and her escort. Jo-Alice felt an unwelcomed chill and then immediately felt silly for her fear. The cat's form came into view out of the shadows. A dingy black cat with white paws and a white tip of the tail. A white triangle began between its eyes and finished at his chin. "Mangy old tom," she said.

"Be careful now, Jo-Alice. Cats can shake a bridge."

"Get out! You are too much, Charles Williams." But she didn't take her eyes off of the cat's eyes to look back at Charles. Something was unnerving about that cat.

"No, I'm serious, Jo-Alice. Cats are creatures that you don't mess with, especially a black cat. If he senses something off by you, he'll show you who is boss by throwing his weight around."

The world was lightening up around them with the rising sun. The cat crept forward, and Jo-Alice could see one of those white paws placed ahead of the other three. The bridge creaked. Jo-Alice's heart dropped.

"Smile at it."

"I ain't smiling at no cat." She watched the cat as it walked closer. The bridge shook. Jo-Alice jumped closer to Charles. "Shit."

"Little girl, I told you."

"I'm not a girl anymore, Charles."

"You acting like one. Just do what I say."

The cat crept closer still, one step, two, three, each white-covered paw moving independently of the others. The bridge shook more.

"Smile, girl," Charles said from behind her.

Jo-Alice, who was now in Charles's arms, smiled. Charles put his arms around her, and the bridge stilled. "Let's go," Charles said. He let her go and walked on the outside so that he would be the one who'd have to share space with the cat as they passed. The two continued to Untethered Lagoon.

2. CATFISH

"You are having problems with your worms," Jo-Alice said. She took the hook from Charles along with the large night crawler he was working with. "Teacher, be taught." She simply baited the hook and gave it back to Charles.

"I'll be damned. You learned fast."

"I didn't learn from you." She was annoyed with her fishing partner, who kept whistling. "You're scaring the fish away, man." She sucked her teeth at him.

Fishing, they both sat on a pier, side by side, with their lines in the water. Charles kept whistling and talking. He kept letting his rough hand rest on Jo-Alice's thigh. "Look here," she said after some time, "I'm going to catch jackshit with you. I'm going down a bit. You stay here." Jo-Alice walked south around the lagoon. It was a small body of water, maybe more of a pond than a lagoon, maybe more of a lake than a pond. The water here was far from the farms and civilization. People who fished here kept it clean and kept it secret. The only other fishers she saw at Untethered were Black like her or the occasional Native American. Her father had told her that when slavery was still in vogue, escapees would stop here first to fish and rinse the smell of plantation and hate from their clothes and bodies.

Now Jo-Alice's line was taut. Something was biting. From experience she knew it was something big. She led it awhile, then pulled. Charles, noisy and clumsy, let go of his own line and came running at her. "I'll help you, baby girl," he said. To herself she said, "If that motherfucker don't stop calling me girl." The thought invigorated her. She pulled and saw that fish face crest the water, whiskers wild and stiff shaking from the force of the line and the water.

"That's a big, muddy bastard," Charles said. He jumped up and down like a tree animal. "Why can't he be still," Jo-Alice thought. She yanked when she should have played, ripping the skin off of her right hand's index finger. But that fish breached the water again. This time a little bit of its body showed through.

"Help or back off, Chuck."

Charles got behind her, and he helped bring it in. It was an ugly thing, as catfish are, but beautiful, too, in its resistance and its size. Its rubbery whiskers crazily whipped the air about him. Its heavy jaws bulged with the audacity of being above water, heavy fish lips flopped open and closed, indignant at the idea of dying, of being somewhere not home, not wet. Its body struggled, and the tail swished as if the fish were swimming in the air. Eyes bulging to capacity. Gasping for breath and hardly breathing.

"Watch that you don't get cut," Charles said, meaning for Jo-Alice to steer clear of its whiskers and rough skin.

Jo-Alice ignored him. She knew catfish. "It's a gorgeous cat, innit?"

"It is. I can't believe you caught the first one."

Why was he ruining the moment?

The fish was easily twenty inches. Almost three pounds. Jo-Alice took it and banged its head against a nearby rock. Its eyes closed against the blow. Shocked-looking fish. See how easy it is to kill, she thought, when you can imagine the taste of it.

"You best go check your line, Charles Williams," she said.

3. CAT

Forty years later, Jo-Alice was at her daughter Nan's house. Nan's kids were visiting with their children. Jo-Alice's two other children, their kids, and their kids were visiting too. Twenty-two people were in her house that day! They were visiting all the way from Georgia, from Tennessee, from Texas and Illinois. She loved the noise and having them around, but she loved it when it was just her, Nan, and Nan's husband.

Jo-Alice was making a pot of spaghetti sauce, stirring in all the ingredients that made it taste good enough to silence those who ate it. This was her own recipe, which was heavily borrowed from her mother and to which she added her own touches, like a shot of bourbon and brown sugar. She would let it simmer all day. That night they would have it with catfish and cornbread. The catfish were caught by her son-in-law and her great-grandsons. Why wouldn't, she wondered, any of the girls go fish with them? "Y'all should go," she told her granddaughters. "Good fishing on those little lagoons beside Lake Michigan," she said.

"Grandma, fishing involves worms, and I ain't about to deal with that." Her granddaughter lit a cigarette from the one in her mouth and traded off. Jo-Alice's great-granddaughters squirmed as if affected by the thought and groaned. "Worms!"

"Worms ain't so bad. I used to fish when I was a kid. Hell, I took you fishing when you were a kid."

"I know. I remember. I hated it then too."

"Go smoke that damn thing somewhere else."

"I liked being with you, Grandma, but the worms!"

"The porch, baby girl, go on with that cigarette."

Jo-Alice left the pot of sauce on simmer and went to retrieve the fish from the bathtub where they rested. With bucket in hand, she went into the downstairs bathroom. There she saw her daughter's mangy cat.

It really wasn't mangy. It was kept clean and was well-fed. Its coat was always sleek and shiny. A tuxedo cat, her daughter called it. Its name was Mr. Cosmopolitan, and they called it Cosmo for short. And Jo-Alice hated it. Or him. Her daughter insisted that she refer to it as a he. She watched Cosmo walk the rim of the bathtub, one white paw placed deftly before the other with each step he took. He was fishing, or so he thought. "Gone, cat," Jo-Alice said. Then she remembered that day on the bridge. Was this why she hated cats?

The cat meowed at her.

"You going to eat your brothers? Because that's what they are, ain't they? Catfish. They named after you."

The cat meowed again. He always tried to sit on her lap when she was in the living room, and she hated that. He always tried to get in her room. She hated getting up in the middle of the night to visit the bathroom, as she had to do more often now with her age, because she'd see Cosmo running around by himself, his eyes glowing in the low light of late night. Hated the hell out of that cat.

"I don't know why y'all named the same," she said, as if Cosmo's meowing questioned her accusation. "Probably because y'all both got whiskers. Stupid reason, if you ask me. Lots of things got whiskers."

Mr. Cosmo meowed again, a long, drawn-out meow that was desperate and loving. Placating almost.

"Can you shake bridges? Hmm?"

Another meow.

Jo-Alice shook her head. "To be young and impressionable, right? Years I've spent with that fool because of his silly lie. And after that, lies, lies, lies. You want some fish, cat? Well, you going to have to wait, just like the rest of us." Alice reached in the tub and got two of the large fish out and put them in her bucket. "Come on, cat. Mr. Cosmopolitan. You going make yourself sick with want."

The cat did come. He watched Alice as she covered the kitchen table with newspaper. He watched her slice the fish just around the gills and cut off the dorsal fin. She cut a long slit along the back and pulled the skin back like a banana peel, but with much more force. He watched her gut the fish and slice it up into fry-able pieces. He rubbed his body against her calf and generally just got more persistent. "Back up now," Jo-Alice told him. When she finished cleaning and cutting those two fish, she went to the tub to get more. Cosmo was right behind her, his white-tipped tail in the air. When she spoke to him, he responded with meows and chirps.

He listened to her stories about fishing in Tennessee as a child, on the Mississippi as a young adult, and in the cool lakes in Wisconsin, where she migrated to in the sixties. "One thing I was afraid of," she said, "coming up here to Wisconsin—that is, besides the cold I was warned about—what worried me was the fishing. I knew there was that big ol' Lake Michigan, but I wasn't sure if there was a good lagoon here or not, or littler lakes."

She lobbed a chunk of catfish guts at Mr. Cosmopolitan, and he caught it before it hit the ground. He ate it graciously. He then went to his water bowl and lapped water from it. Jo-Alice watched the cat, feeling more affection for him. "I must be getting ready to die," she said.

Later, when she fried the fish up, she fried him a special unbreaded piece. The family was surprised to see her drop the choice piece in the cat's bowl.

They all sat down, sixteen members of the family, to a plate of cornbread, white dinner rolls, spaghetti, and fish fried in cornmeal and seasoning.

"You seen a ghost or something, Mama?" her daughter asked.

"What you talking about?" Jo-Alice asked back.

"Feeding Mr. Cosmo like you turned over a new leaf or talked to someone about the love of animals. You not getting soft on me, are you?"

"I ain't seen nothing." She watched the cat eat the chunk of fish she had made just for him. He started off quickly, his jaws working to keep the food in his mouth. Then he slowed down, seemingly savoring every bite that came. Satisfied herself, Jo-Alice begin to eat her fish too. "I'm just steadying some bridges."

Tooth Fairy

"I sometimes hurt where teeth used to be," Carson said. He then reached into his mouth, toward the back, his pinky in the air as if he were holding a fine china teacup. Then he pulled out a molar and placed it on the table between us. Spots of white gleamed through the rot. Blood clung to the root. The waitress came and refilled our coffees, and I couldn't look at her. I still wonder if she saw that tooth.

"Thank you," I said to the waitress. She didn't say anything back.

A second later, Carson was pouring sugar into his coffee. The waitress left us. "Coffee's a bitter drink," he said.

"You going back home ever?"

He stopped pouring the sugar and took a sip. "Fuck for? I mean what is home now?" He put air quotes around *home*. I could see his tongue working its way over his teeth behind his mouth. Carson had recently lost his only son to gun violence. He was still married, and he still had other children, but Carson Jr.'s death left a dearth of possibility for him. The football games, the prom, the college acceptance letter. Junior was a local rock star, but now he was gone. Wasn't even involved in that life, just caught in the crossfire.

"Where are you going?"

He picked up his coffee and was going to drink again, but he shook his head and put the mug back down. "Did I ever tell you about North Dakota?"

"Nah, you haven't. What's the word?"

"Oil. In fucking North Dakota. And you can make a killing working for them."

"So you ain't talking about going out there and prospecting."

"What I look like? I just need a job. Maybe if I could go away for a while, a couple of years there maybe, make some serious money."

"Send some back to Rosie, right?" I asked.

"Hell yes. I mean, she still my wife. And the girls."

"After a couple of years then. Will you go back home after?"

Carson reached a shaking finger out to his discarded tooth. He held the finger over the tooth but didn't touch it. "I can't, Morrie. Maybe by then, I can send for Rosie and the girls."

"Maybe." I sat back in the booth. Carson stopped playing with his tooth. He sat back, too, stretched out and yawned, rubbed his exposed belly. "You should come with me. Out west."

"What? Nah, man, I won't fit in."

"What you saying?"

"How many Black men you think are in North Dakota?"

"With you there will be at least one."

"I'm not looking to be a statistic."

"It's damn good money, Morrie." Carson looked out the window. From there you could see my jeep, a real army one I bought at a surplus auction. I didn't see the vehicle that got Carson there; I'm guessing he took the bus. He was still looking out the window past the parking lot, his expression a mixture of grief and something like desperation.

It was as good a time as any to excuse myself. I stood up, took a twenty out of my pocket, and placed it on the table next to his tooth. "I wish you all the best."

He looked at the money with a smirk, but he made no move to reject it or to find money in his own pockets. "That's eighteen more than what the coffee's worth."

"Then just call me the Tooth Fairy," I said.

Out in my jeep, I looked in the rearview at my own smile. Grimaced in the sunlight. My mostly intact teeth shined back. Not bad. I counted each and every one of my blessings. I sat back in the seat and considered how many more blessings I'd want. North Dakota sounded cold and white, and I tried to imagine oil rigs and pumping jacks on a prairie that wasn't Texas. Not that I knew much about Texas either. What would you do if you work for oil? How safe would it be? How much money could you earn?

I started the engine, and the smell of the exhaust hit right away. I could use better money, I knew, but if I wasn't making it in Milwaukee, why would I make it farther west in a whiter place? Even with his lack of education and teeth, I knew Carson would have a better chance than me anywhere he went.

"But the possibilities," I said. I turned on my stereo and heard the music I'd heard a million times before, the beats from it bleeding in with the beats from countless other songs. I turned the radio off and left the parking lot, trying to remember what I knew about North Dakota.

Carry the Weight

After the din died down and mostly everyone had left, Cary watched as his wife, Mary Beth, stumbled around with a red wine glass full of something clear, trying her best to appear sober. She was explaining in her best college English, articulating her consonants clearly, why she had fallen down earlier that evening. She was also speculating why her crocheted shawl was ripped at the hem. He had told her not to wear it. He had told her to wear more sensible shoes, to which she sneered and nearly cried because was Cary calling her old? "I still can wear pumps to a party," she said, accentuating her Ps. Was she, even then, already tipsy? And now she was far gone.

He'd have to coax her to calm down.

He imagined carrying her home.

Cary watched Mary Beth carefully prance around the Cheethams' apartment, dodging the sharp edges of end tables and midcentury couch legs, and realized that his wife had a problem. Not only was she a drunk, but she was an ordinary drunk. Her progression through the disease was as commonplace as a baby's development into toddlerhood and beyond: first words, first steps, potty-trained, and so on. And when kids decide who they are, that wouldn't be much different from a million other teenagers or young adults on this planet.

"Mary Beth," he said, "it's fine. You didn't hurt anyone. You didn't hurt yourself." His wife looked at him with feigned shock, as bad a front as her performed sobriety. She behaved like a classic alcoholic.

This banality of life oppressed Cary. He wanted some deviation. Maybe, he wondered, he was the exception. Maybe he was someone special. The thought of himself being anything other than a software engineer making decent money for a decent life made him laugh out loud: he was as nameless as his profession.

"You're laughing at me," Mary Beth said, the indignity moving from play to actual injury.

"Honey, I'm not." Cary stood up. "I'm laughing at myself." He took his wife's elbow and half-steered her to the hallway leading out of the apartment. "Let's get going, okay? We've both had a lot to drink."

"You did not," she said. "You have to drive us home."

Cary nodded. "I do." He grabbed Mary Beth's purse from the hall tree and handed it to her. He wanted to believe that he was breaking whatever rut they were in that made life feel predetermined. Maybe stopping this drunken explanation before Mary Beth got sick and/or passed out at the Cheethams' would end it, end her foray into alcoholism. But then what? How would Mary Beth emerge from that path?

"Let's wish Phil and Tayesicha good night," he said. He took Mary Beth's elbow and guided her again, this time to find the hosts.

Both Phil and Tayesicha gave Mary Beth a concerned but judgmental look. They interrupted their conversation with three others in the kitchen. "Are you guys taking off?" Phil asked. "Are you okay?" Tayesicha asked Mary Beth.

Mary Beth burped quietly and excused herself. None of them was anything remarkable, Cary thought.

PART IV

Your house is on fire
And your children all gone

—MOTHER GOOSE

Now the doctor's gonna do all that he can
But what you're gonna need
is an undertaker man

—MAMIE SMITH,
"Crazy Blues"

Ladybird, Ladybird

Birdlike. Flitting? Bouncy? Do I float? "It's that you're light. You peck at your food. Hollow bones."

"My bones aren't hollow."

"No," he shakes his head. "No, I know they're not. But it is like they're hollow. You know. Like a bird."

"Avian."

He shrugs. "Sure."

I imagine him dying.

I imaging taking one of my chopsticks and turning it away from the deep-fried tofu and toward him. I see myself forcing its dull tip into his chest, breaking beyond errant bones and stringent skin, plunging through to his heart. Maybe both chopsticks? I am diving in and sawing at his heart, using the sticks as knives, picking up juicy bits of his heart. "Your voice too" he says.

"My voice?"

"Singsongy. See, you just asked a question there."

"Well, I didn't know."

"But your voice goes up and down. Like a melody that doesn't mean anything."

I put my chopsticks down. Suddenly I don't feel like Chinese food. I don't feel like food. I want to keep eating because I'm afraid that he'll continue the metaphor, but I can't eat. His heart blood is all over the eggplant and tofu, the steamed brown rice, the noodles— it's on everything. I can't tell what's red pepper and what's him. I cannot eat this. I say: "You remember that chant? About the bird? 'Fly away home. Your house is on fire. Your children are alone."

He asks: "Do you want children?"

I think about the term *fall out of love with*. I had always called bullshit. I never believed that people could fall out of love like people could fall in love.

But here I am. Falling as if my wings are clipped.

Whisper Network

On Monday, Venessa Stenson stared out the window during math drills. Mrs. Reynolds called to her, asked her for the solution in the problem set, and waited for an answer. Venessa looked at Mrs. Reynolds and shook her head slightly. "I don't know," she said. Her voice was breathier than usual, lower. Venessa turned away and looked back out the window. Mrs. Reynolds thought to scold the girl but noted something in her demeanor that said sadness, so she went on. She called on Bobby instead, who eagerly gave the right answer.

Tuesday, over optional breakfast, Mrs. Reynolds saw Venessa whispering into Melody's ear. Mrs. Reynolds watched as Melody's mood changed. The child seemed to deflate: her little face caved in, and her brow burrowed deep into her eyes. Angrily, Mrs. Reynolds marched toward the girls, sure that Venessa had told Melody something mean, but again she was met by the melancholy of Venessa and stopped. Maybe Venessa's grandmother died. Or her cat. It was always horrible when pets died.

By social studies hour, four girls were near tears: Venessa, Melody, Cindy, and Samantha. They didn't sit near each other. They sat in four different sections of the classroom, and each one of them looked off into space. Mrs. Reynolds called to the lesser one, Cindy: "Pay attention. The capital of Uruguay, Cindy."

Cindy looked at Mrs. Reynolds, her big blue eyes wet and hurt. "It's Montevideo, Mrs. Reynolds." She then looked away, her small head framed by amber curls. Dead cat, thought Mrs. Reynolds.

Wednesday, at lunch, Mrs. Reynolds watched girl after girl whisper into another girl's ear. Some were in her class; some were in Mrs. Garcia's class or Ms. Hayes's class. She leaned over now to the other two women and asked, "What is it with our girls?"

"What do you mean?" Ms. Hayes asked. "Hey, do you have any cigarettes left? I ran out."

"I do," Mrs. Garcia said.

"But you smoke menthol."

"Look, if you're really fiending for nicotine, you wouldn't care. You want one? Meet me on the west side at recess. I'll spot you."

"Listen—it's mostly the boys talking," Mrs. Reynolds said. The three women all went quiet as if listening for an odd noise in the middle of the night.

"I hear some girls," Mrs. Garcia said.

Ms. Hayes nodded and looked around. "But Becky's right. It's mostly boys, innit? Odd. You think it's some kind of game?"

"I see them whispering," Mrs. Reynolds said. "One whispers to the other, then they are both just, I don't know, crestfallen."

The three teachers watched as Samantha, who recently went through a growth spurt and was about a half-foot taller than her classmates, walked over to Shalonda, who was in Ms. Hayes's class.

Samantha asked Shalonda something, and Shalonda responded. Then, conspiratorially, Samantha leaned over, moved some of Shalonda's box braids away from her ear, and whispered something.

"Shalonda's tough," Ms. Hayes said. "This won't affect her."

Shalonda nodded. Then Samantha stood up straight, towering over the other girl. Her face was red from bending over, but still she looked pale.

"Watch," Ms. Hayes said. Shalonda looked as if she was not fazed, as if she had just heard a mediocre joke. Samantha walked away. "See?"

They continued to watch Shalonda to learn if the girl was not infected by the whisper campaign. For a full minute, Shalonda did nothing but spin her fidget spinner. Then the girl kind of collapsed into herself. Her lips drew down, and her nose folded into it, forcing a squinched-up scowl. Shalonda bent at the waist, and her knees buckled beneath her. She didn't cry, but she may as well have.

"Maybe a story about a pet dying?" Mrs. Reynolds said.

"That's ridiculous," Mrs. Garcia argued.

"Cats are important."

"Nothing as little as a cat," Mrs. Garcia said. "Maybe someone's grandma or maybe their whole family. You think murder-suicide?"

Ms. Hayes said: "Stop reading the news. It could be something bigger than that, something more philosophical. Something existential. Maybe they realize that, ultimately, none of this matters."

"What do you mean none of this?"

"I mean fourth grade. Fractions and solving for x. Capitals of countries and understanding puberty. Maybe they now know that they'll learn all of this shit, march through the requirements, and die anyway."

"We keep saying dying," Mrs. Reynolds said. "Maybe it's us. Maybe they look at us and see droopy boobs, sagging asses, and crow's-feet crisscrossing our eyes and lips."

"Speak for yourself, babe," Ms. Hayes said. "Ain't nothing sagging on me."

Mrs. Garcia rolled her eyes at her younger colleague. "Maybe," she began, but the bell rang. They moved toward the front of the lunchroom near the doors and blew whistles, calling for the children to line up. As the fourth graders got in place and the three teachers and their aides marched them outside for recess, Mrs. Garcia's *maybe* rang through the stale lunchroom.

Wednesday night Mrs. Reynolds told her husband about the girls. Over dinner—mashed potatoes, roast beef, corn, and a wedge salad—Mr. Reynolds said, "Maybe it's a trick they're all playing. A little kid's equivalent to a flash mob."

"What do you mean?" she asked her husband.

"I mean that they're not really sad, but they are acting to see how the world around them reacts. Are all of the girls doing this?"

"Nearly so, but only in fourth grade."

"The girls who are not, are they unpopular?"

"No. I think they just haven't gotten the secret yet. I'm telling you, Malcolm, it's like an infection or something." Mrs. Reynolds put her knife and fork down. She wasn't eating.

"I'm sure by next week it will be fine."

She thought about the girls getting older, getting breasts and menses, getting pregnant and fat, getting felt up or raped, getting passed over. "Have you noticed the lines on my face getting deeper?"

Mr. Reynolds stuffed a forkful of meat and potatoes into his mouth. He shook his head no, not looking up at his wife.

"Cathy thinks the girls are having a collective existential crisis."

Mr. Reynolds laughed, spewing potatoes all over his plate and Mrs. Reynolds's hand. Mrs. Reynolds stood up from the table, washed her hands at the kitchen sink, and held back tears as her husband continued to laugh.

Recess on Thursday was a boisterous time for the fourth-grade boys. They had the run of the playground, and there they were, trying to swing as high as possible on the swings, and when they reached those heights, they'd jump off. They boogied across the monkey bars, playing chicken by scissoring each other's legs and trying to make each other jump off. They ran up and down the slides and spun the tire swing at sickening revolutions. They threw a football throughout the playground and tackled each other without mercy.

The girls stood listlessly off toward the doors to the school, not talking, not giggling, not smiling. They looked pitiful. "We grow older, then old," Ms. Hayes was saying, "then we get useless and become burdens. We die. Most of us won't be remembered beyond our immediate families and our friends, and when they die, we'll be forgotten completely. Gravestones marking our existences for no one at all."

"Would you stop it with that? Garcias do not become burdens. We love and care for our old. We remember each other in celebration during Día de Muertos; we live forever."

"Bullshit, Esmeralda. You're not even a practicing Catholic!"

"Día de Muertos existed well before the Spaniards came over. Whatever, Tina, the point I was trying to make is that's not what's wrong with those girls. I think it has to do with the shootings."

"What shootings?"

"All the shootings! The gangs around here. The cops killing Black and brown kids. They are upset at their fathers beating their mothers, their big brothers not getting jobs, their big sisters getting pregnant. You don't know about these things because you go back home to the 'burbs at night."

"The 'burbs.' Are you fucking kidding me?"

"Ladies," Mrs. Reynolds said, holding up her hand. She pointed at one of the boys who was playing football, running backward, not watching his step, and along the trajectory of a girl. Yelling,

"Watch it," Mrs. Reynolds ran to protect the girl, but she was too late. The backward-running boy bumped into the girl at top speed. The impact was audible. The girl—a medium-height and weight girl from Mrs. Garcia's class—went down. She did not hold her arms and hands out to protect herself but fell flat on her face. The girl emotionlessly turned her head to the side so that she was not kissing dirt. Mrs. Reynolds could see that the child was bleeding and needed some attention, but the kid had not even cried. She just stayed there, on the ground, looking at nothing at all.

"Are you all right?" Mrs. Reynolds asked. The child closed and opened her eyes really slowly. Fishlike.

"Renee?" Mrs. Garcia called out as she walked toward the girl and Mrs. Reynolds. Figuring it was her friend's student and she needed to see the boy who collided with her, Mrs. Reynolds stood up and heard, "Watch out!" She was hit by a football below and beneath her shoulder blades, along the spine. Her arms buckled, and her body shifted forward. Tears stung her eyes, but of course, she did not cry, not in front of her students. "Hey!" she said. She turned around and saw laughing men, moving about in spite of hurt and stagnant women—she turned again and saw stunned but jittery boys. There were no men. What was she supposed to say to them? To stop playing? To pay attention to the quiet girls? To ask why?

At home that night, she lay silently beneath her husband, her hands kindly grasping his shoulders, but her mind was with the girls and their crusade of misery. It was not what Mrs. Garcia or Ms. Hayes thought but something else, something more primal. These girls were probably anticipating a lifetime of their bodies being vessels for other people, from partners to progeny. They probably were aware of all that women came to be, the strides they've made, so to speak, but see them being stymied by systemic sexism. They probably saw the freedom of the boys on the playground tossing a football and all that the almond-shaped ball represented: wars fought and won, organization, camaraderie, all that was for men. American women historically were made to be loners: at kitchen, at dining table, at sewing, and now, at work. Wouldn't a secretary pool at least allow women to be adjacent to each other (were they allowed to speak)? In spite of being in front of thirty people all day and having nearly a hundred colleagues, she herself had always felt isolated.

And what of her profession? How many men held her position at her school? The men there were the gym teachers, the health teachers, the counselors, and the principals.

Her husband finished, and she, so wrapped up in her thoughts, did not notice, missed her cue to make noises. He rolled off of her and lay beside her. "I don't think you have anything to worry about. Next week they will be back to normal."

"Would that be good? To just go back to how they were before? Would they have learned anything?"

"Are they learning anything from this?"

Mrs. Reynolds sat up, not wanting to say another thing to Mr. Reynolds about her fourth graders. "Maybe they aren't the ones who need enlightenment."

"What the fuck is that supposed to mean?"

Mrs. Reynolds got out of bed.

Friday morning Mrs. Reynolds took a short shower. She didn't fix her braids. She wore no makeup and packed a bag of family-sized potato chips for lunch. At school she had her students do group work and watched as the boys took over and reluctantly took the notes. The girls looked macabre in their doldrums. Their faces were all twisted in some state of disgust. Their hair was uncombed, fuzzy; they were all carelessly beautiful.

At recess both Mrs. Garcia and Ms. Hayes were unprepared for the world, dressed down in jeans and T-shirts, hair messy and faces unmade. Ms. Hayes openly smoked right there on the playground, beneath the DRUG FREE ZONE sign. None of the three women smiled. Their faces sagged into the expressions they used when they were alone, when no one was watching, when there was no reason to care.

"It occurs to me," Mrs. Reynolds said, "that we've never asked the girls what was wrong."

Ms. Hayes lit another cigarette from the butt of her first cigarette. Mrs. Garcia grabbed the pack from Ms. Hayes and shook a cigarette out. Mrs. Reynolds had another handful of sour cream and onion potato chips. "It's so gorgeous outside today," she said.

Back in her class, the boys wouldn't quite quiet down, wouldn't stop shifting in their seats, couldn't really refrain from making paper airplanes and spitballs with notebook paper, and they couldn't prevent both the airplanes and the spitballs from flying through the air. No one, not even Mrs. Reynolds, was paying attention to the lecture. The girls were silent but distant and down. Venessa Stenson stifled something, and Mrs. Reynolds stopped. "Venessa," she said.

Venessa looked at her, her eyes full of water, but she wasn't crying.

"Venessa, what is wrong?"

The girl's face crumbled into agony. Her mouth opened, and she let go of a sob. This is a sound, Mrs. Reynolds thought. She made a sound! And with that, Mrs. Reynolds felt guilty for never contacting the girls' parents—this girl or any of the girls. How had they behaved at home? Were they as sullen there as they were in school? Was this a citywide epidemic? Were girls wandering around town mute and morose? And why hadn't any parents contacted her?

"What is wrong?"

Venessa cried harder, not wiping her face of the tears that fell. Her hands stayed in her lap, and her head shook with the sobs, but the girl did not move. Mrs. Reynolds asked again, "What is wrong with you, Venessa?" And the other girls began to cry.

By Monday would it be back to normal? Had Mrs. Reynolds wanted that? She left the classroom in search of her friends Mrs. Garcia and Ms. Hayes, leaving behind paper projectiles and tears, raucous boy noise. Leaving behind the sobbing girls.

The Ballad of Frankie Baker

Frankie Baker, gray as a Missouri storm, stood so tall, the room grew close. She yelled, "He wasn't named no Johnny. You listening to those songs on the Victrola and the radio. His name was Allen, and he was nothing but a struggling, loser pimp who I thought loved me." She swiftly moved from anger to tears; her sobs came quick and transformed her to a small, lesser thing. She was now a woman who put too much of herself into a prospect worth nothing. "Guess you'd call me his whore. But he was mine. My man! He played piano."

She sat down and turned away from us. Her tired, black hand reached up and caressed the padded walls. Then the other hand joined in. Her fingers played invisible notes, her left hand striding along the lower register. "Ragtime. It was still fairly new. He made up songs too."

She stopped playing her soft piano, then turned to us, looked at us over her shoulder. "The girl wasn't named Nellie Bly. That's them Victrola and radio y'all hearing. She was another whore. And

I didn't shoot him there. I shot him at home because he tried to stab me. I shot him as God would have me do. That's why I'm still alive. I'm a Christian woman."

Miss Baker pulled a folded-up piece of newsprint from her bosom. She caringly unfolded it. "They all got it wrong," she said. "I was nice and thick. Beautiful." She passed me the sheet, and I saw a print of the Thomas Hart Benton painting. "That woman they depicted there is as thin as a whisper. She shoots Allen in his back. I shot that motherfucker in the chest a couple of times. He too evil to die right away. And look at that woman. That's how they make us look. That wasn't me! I was beautiful."

I gave her the engraving back.

"I had curls," she said.

Three Studies in Patience

I. BIRD DOG

Worms were for birds with limited perspectives. Let them wake early. Let them eat worms. Woodstock waits for bigger game, impossible food from fools who lie unaware of impending doom. What bigger dunce than a dog who sleeps atop his home instead of inside, safe from the likes of preying birds? What bigger fool to proffer a belly fattened with gifted food and an easy life?

Woodstock's game was a long one. He pretended to befriend the beast so he can be close without suspicion. Snoopy was cow adjacent. When real hunger hits him, Woodstock will rise and get his worm.

II. A KIND OF NOURISHMENT

They are just vitamins, but they are chewy between the molars, leaking medicinal orange, grape, and cherry flavors. She feeds the fun shapes to her husband as if they were candy. He asks for more, and she gives him more. She wonders how long will it take until the diarrhea starts, for his heart to beat faster. She thinks of the word *toxicity* and how toxic is toxic enough.

At night she feeds him green potatoes with eyes of the tubers, pulverized and covered in brown gravy. Fruit punch laced with crushed apple seeds. She serves dinner with a wifely smile.

III. AT LEAST ONE THOUSAND CUTS

Blame him. Kate Idaho did. He asked for sex all the time because that's how he knew how to speak. She gave it because she knew it took from him. And she'd notch his back in tally marks with her index fingernail, waiting for his ailing, aging body to give into the stress she exerted on his bones.

Kate Idaho liked to bring him near climax from above, then leap off him as if ejected. She'd then run around the condo, imagining the dimples at the top of her ass catching the light. She'd feel all the fleshy parts of herself jingling with each footfall. Silly Fred would chase her as if he could take the exertion.

His breathing would be so spent toward the end. He could hardly catch his breath. Kate would let him catch her and then fuck him fast, bringing him to finish.

And then what, she wondered? Once he was gone? They weren't married, so it was not for the money. She didn't care about the money, though she'd probably get her share.

But that was the *then what*, and she understood it from the start: the satisfaction of knowing how it would feel to kill a man.

PART V

The sky hangs heavy tonight
Like the hair of a Negro woman.

—LEWIS GRANDISON ALEXANDER,
"Negro Woman"

It is fitting that you be here
Little brown boys

—LANGSTON HUGHES,
"On Seeing Two Brown Boys
in a Catholic Church"

For I was born on Saturday—
    "Bad time for planting a seed"

—COUNTEE CULLEN,
"Saturday's Child"

Going Home

Three boys left the corner store run by men who spoke English only to their customers. The boys' pockets bulged with what used to be called penny candy but now cost too much to justify such a name. They each had twenty ounces of soda filled with caffeine and sugar in one hand and a grab bag size of chips in the other. One's hair was curly, one's hair was French braided into cornrows, and one's hair was clipped close to the scalp with a neatly professional, clear part on the left side. They spoke in shortened sentences. They quoted lines from action films. Their arms and legs were long and black, one so black he shone in the sun. Like pendulums, their limbs swung to a rhythm of some clock.

And this is how they disappeared:

The one with curly hair (and with caterpillar eyelashes) saw a girl who was at least three inches taller than himself. He felt warmth, an uncomfortable warmth, a warmth like the urine running down his legs when he was in third grade while he stood in the corner for not doing something wrong when the teacher's back was turned.

Now his friends barely nodded at his knees buckling beneath him, hardly waved or said a word when he walked away. Though the boy with the cornrows watched him trot after the girl—he watched, more, the girl who was the color of the sun when it's nearing its zenith, the color of dough just before it's bread. He watched her dissipate into the dust. He watched his friend follow.

If someone could have asked the cornrowed boy about his friend who left, he would not have known what to say. How do you translate desire as desperate as that? His gait slowed, even for a Black boy who was too cool for his own momentum to go forward, so his friend with the close-cropped hair moved on, ahead of him. The wind blew from the east, from Lake Michigan, over him, over his hair, through the parted waves of rows along his scalp that exposed the skin, the same skin that perspired in the summer sun. He cooled then. He felt cold all over. He poured chips flaming and salty down his throat. He coughed, spat out red, and assured himself it wasn't blood. It was Red Lake No. 40 and Yellow No. 5 coloring all his dreams the wrong shade. He watched his friend with his nearly bald head, moving on. But had he himself stopped moving, the boy with cornrows wondered? He took a step forward. Shivered. He had stopped moving. He couldn't bring himself to take another step. His cheek, now covered in ice, cracked. The shattered surfaces of him shimmered like so many diamonds in the gleaming sun. Juicy, wet droplets of him cascaded to the warm concrete and gathered and then ran into the grate.

The last boy was big. He had diabetes, and he had no fear. He reached into his pocket and pulled out melted chocolate. He ate it, licking the side of his hand where the chocolate, almost as dark as his skin, melted down. He drank his soda. His head, both cool and hot, dripped water. Droplets covered his scalp. He turned and looked at his friend frozen in place. He thought to call for him but stopped himself. Why should his friend move? Where would walking take him? He watched the frozen boy with cornrows for a while, watched his skin melt in the sun, and finished his bag of chips, which were "cool ranch" flavored. He didn't know what *cool ranch* was. Was that a place? Was that a restaurant? What was a ranch? Were there cows or horses on a ranch? How did this taste—this flavor of salt and sour and herbs—perform ranch-ness? And why a cool ranch? He shook the bits of crumbs and seasoning (mostly salt, so much salt) down his throat and threw the empty bag down on the ground.

And how did he disappear?

Let's say he ran away. Let's say he choked on salt and sweet. Let's say that he grew old after marrying and after fathering children. Let's say that he didn't disappear.

But he did. The question he asked of his friend—why should he move—irked him into his own immobility. He still had candy, and he still had soda, but he didn't want it. Did he stop too? No, he simply worried himself into the ground.

Black boys disappear every day.

The Negotiation of Space

ONE

A tree was floating in the lake. Ira watched it as it bobbed on the waves, forward toward them and back to the breakwaters. The lake was colored slate blue, and ashy waters crashed together beneath an overcast sky. When they had started their day, the clouds began sparse and small, but now the clouds were fat globs of foreboding. "They're bringing on a storm," Dana said. She sat on a park bench and watched the waters. Her face, along with the lake, changed colors as the day grew longer.

"Dana, you don't look so good."

"It's funny, Ira, but I think I got seasick while on shore. Silly, right?"

Ira looked out at the lake again. The tree was treading water westward now, moving toward The Home. He pictured it on the lawn, waiting for them when they returned. He imagined, too, a few rocks smoothed from years in the water—decades—smooth like something newly birthed, on the steps leading up to the home. "The problem, Dana, is that everything here is curly like the waves. The rocks, that tree, everything looks to be moving. How can you stay still in that? Let's walk, honey, along the shore. Let's go get the van."

"Ira, we missed the van fifteen minutes ago. I told you. I told you to get a move on or we'll have to take the bus."

"There is nothing wrong with the bus."

Ira and Dana were old people. Dana had always been pale, veins prominent across the flat plane of her forehead, on the bridge of her nose near her eyes, on the back of her hands, and on the inside of her wrists. Her fair skin reminded Ira that she was both alive and constantly dying. Seeing Dana there, in front of Lake Michigan teeming with some unknown anger at some unknown thing, her skin changing from her usual high ecru tone to a sickness-induced coral color, Ira couldn't help but think of Monet contemplating the hues of his wife's skin as she died.

"Oh," Dana said, sitting further back on the bench. She was a big woman: broad shoulders and hips, hefty thighs and strong legs. Ira feared having to carry her along the beach, looking for a bus stop, then waiting for the bus to come, helping her onto the bus. He could call for a taxi, but that would be too dear for them. He looked at her as she placed her head between her legs, the classic pose for nausea. She made a noise as if pushing something heavy or lifting it up.

"Dana," Ira said, taking position slightly beside her and slightly behind her. He held her hair, pressing her curls loosely against her skin, getting the hair out of her way. "Will you be okay?"

She groaned again, this time a long, rumbling sound. Ira felt frustrated in helplessness; he could do nothing further than holding her hair out of her face should she throw up. He straightened slightly and looked around. The others from the retirement home were gone, so Dana was right: the van had left.

"The van should be around again in another fifteen minutes or so," he said. "Didn't they say that? We don't have to take a bus."

"Half an hour," Dana whispered. "The van'll be back in half an hour."

"Should I call someone?"

Dana shook her head once. "Be okay," she said.

Ira was glad because he didn't think he had his phone. He straightened again and saw a young woman walking toward them. Broad hips and determined walk, she looked confident in her abilities. "Ma'am," Ira called out, "are you a nurse?"

The woman slowed and looked at him and Dana. "Excuse me?"

"A nurse?" Ira said. He had begun to see his mistake. "We need a nurse. We need help."

"Ira," Dana said.

"Is it because I'm a Black woman you think I'm a nurse?" She stopped completely and stood on the sidewalk facing Ira and Dana. She had one hand, folded into a fist, on her hip, and the other held a purse and a couple of shopping bags.

Was it because she was Black? Most of his nurses were either Black or what he assumed was Mexican. There was probably some truth in her question but not entirely. "I don't think that's it," Ira said. "You move—" he started, but he heard what he was going to say in his mind and decided against finishing.

"What you need?" the woman asked. She seemed bothered but not unfriendly.

"You're wearing white," he said.

"It's June."

"Your name?"

"No, I mean it's the month of June. I'm celebrating the first day of the month by wearing white."

Ira looked at her. She wore a demi-cardigan and close-fitting pants. Her thighs pushed against the fabric of her pants, and Ira could see the cellulite pocketed there. She looked like a nurse wearing a uniform.

Slower and louder, "What you need?" the young woman said again.

"My wife, Dana, she's not doing too good. We were walking along the shore here. There was a group of us, but many of the residents left on the first van back—and Dana and me—Dana's my wife. Did I tell you she's named Dana?"

The woman puckered her lips out at him, as if pouting in anger. Or as if she had better things to do.

"Ira, leave her," Dana said.

"We sat, Dana and I, on the pier down east a little farther and watched the waves. You ever do that?"

"She feeling dizzy?"

Ira turned to his wife and asked, "Dana, honey, you're dizzy?"

"I hear her, Ira. Of course I'm feeling dizzy."

"Well, you doing the right thing by holding your head down like that. Y'all got a phone?"

"We only really call each other. We left our phones back at the home."

"Ira, I thought you grabbed yours." Dana sounded annoyed.

"I forgot it, honey. I was in a rush, I suppose."

The woman sighed with annoyance and mumbled something under her breath about white people. She walked toward Ira and Dana and looked at them as if they were lacking in intelligence. She sat down on the bench. "I ain't got no car, but I can call somebody. And I ain't no nurse."

The woman sat her bags on the bench between her and Dana. She opened her purse and dug through it for her phone. "I got things to do, but I'm a good woman," she said. "A Christian."

Her hair was braided in tight, little braids that she kept back with a headband. They were long braids, and Ira doubted if it was all her hair. He may be old, but he knew women endowed what they already had. As the woman looked for her phone, Ira looked closer at her braids—one braid, really. She eventually landed on her phone and sat up with it in her hand. She caught Ira staring at her. She narrowed her eyes at him. "What do y'all want? Me to call someone to come get you two? An ambulance or one of y'all kids?"

"Dana and I never had any kids. We both worked hard, you know. We both were into each other. We still are."

Dana stood up abruptly and went to the rough, craggy rocks along the waters. The woman and Ira watched Dana go and then looked modestly away when she threw up. Ira waited a minute, then looked back and saw his wife's back convulse with the force of her illness. It reminded him of pantomime because he could not hear her over the waters and traffic but only see her.

"I have kids," the woman said. "Two girls and a boy. Memphis is the oldest one, then there's Samantha and Jafaru, my baby boy. If y'all want, you can take one of mine! I'm kidding, of course. Where's the retirement home?"

Ira told her the address, and she nodded. "I'm sure she just seasick or something," the woman said. "You watch the waters like that, it can give you the feeling of being out there without being out there. When I was little, I used to love that feeling. My grandmother would take us fishing out on the lagoon, and afterward we'd walk down to the real lake and watch the waters. I'd wait until it get quiet, you know, for my brothers to wander off and my grandmother to stop humming. She'd sit there smoking her cigarettes, and I let the quiet overtake me and watch the waters. I felt like I was moving. Look at the tree out there. Must've broke off from shore up a ways."

Ira reached out and took one of the woman's braids into his hands. He held the plait between his thumb and forefinger and felt the smooth, patterned bumps of hair that made it up. He studied the hair being woven in and out of itself. Where does her hair end, he wondered, and the other hair begin? The woman, surprised, jerked at first but sat still and let the old man hold onto her braid.

TWO

This is what a prisoner looks like:

I. Suspicious of every movement, including your movements, though you are her guest.

II. Small even if she is huge. Her whole body made little by the large, empty rooms she wanders; her workwoman's hands that could deftly wield both sledgehammers and rattail combs are now helpless and useless. They hang from her wrists, which dangle from polyester cuffs.

III. The colors of her clothes—not prison-issued orange jumpsuits, as you expected, but T-shirts and sweaters, painter's pants and tennis shoes—are too primary. Nothing is branded; still you think Dickies.

IV. Though you can imagine nothing but time to sleep there, or time to rest, to think, to consider why you are there, she looks worn-out. She looks older, though it's only been weeks, not years.

V. Hungry and desperate like the want you see on downtown street corners. Without asking, she is asking you. With an affected dignity, like the veterans who sell the cheapest No. 2 pencils and newspapers with news stories written by the homeless, she is asking you.

VI. You remember, when she was free, her hair was straightened weekly: blow dryer, flat iron, and if she wanted to look really good, pressing comb for the front edges. Product fragrance and the stink of singed hair melded with the odors of fried chicken with collard and mustard greens. You remember her hair when you first see her, carefully curled with a roller set and curling iron. When she was still free, people always were telling you your mother had movie star hair. It was soft then, and when you held her, your face in her hair, your chest against her chest, she filled you out.

VII.   She is quieted by the noise around her, including the noises you make. You and she ask each other to repeat what was just said. You lean in close. She smells different—you note this. And sometimes she is loud. She yells laughter. She looks embarrassed after laughing. She checks her lap.

VIII. Skin: tight.

IX.   Her eyes search everywhere around her, constant curiosity, constant checking.

X.   Her hair is French braided into neat little cornrows. It's a masculine style, you think. It's how you sometimes wear your hair. You imagine someone who looks just like your mother braiding your mother's hair. They talk about their children (you are mentioned). They talk about who is new there and who is very old. They talk about who died there and who would die. You think again: rattail comb; she hasn't said much, but she wants to say much more.

Look at her: she has so much to tell you. She cries without buildup. A loud and rude choking sound your mother makes, interrupting all the other prisoners and their sons, daughters, mothers, husbands, lovers, friends. "Mama," you say. She shakes her head. Her face covered now in tears and snot and saliva. "I am," she said, "so tired." She stutters. You reach out, and a guard moves in closer. You close your eyes, and you see your mother sitting on a metal bunk bed, mattress flat and insufficient. She is taking her hair down. The French braids leave thick, defined curls all over her head in neat little cornrows. Or cotton rows. Rows of black, coarse cotton.

You touch her hair. The guard begins to walk over.

THREE

The nurse lifted the baby up and looked at him. All babies were ugly at this point: heads smashed in and covered in goo. She didn't know that yet. This was her first baby. This baby screamed at the audacity of being pulled into the world. She smiled at him. He pissed on her. She smiled wider and laughed. She would take his measurements, bathe him, and give him to his mother again to be held and to suckle.

Later, as the mother slept, the nurse went to the baby and picked him up. Thick, fluffy hair covered his head in loose curls. She reached out and touched it. Felt no different than a white baby's hair. How was it, she wondered, when they aged, their hair gets coarser? Kinkier? What was it that made their hair different?

She stroked the baby's hair, still called Boy Johnson because his mother was sure she was having a girl, and considered the word *kinky*. Was that still okay? Could she say Black people had kinky hair?

FOUR

His beard, coarse and black, hung stiffly from his chin. I wanted to run my fingers through it, get tangled up in it, tangibly tangled up in him. I played stalker at work until he noticed me. "Wherever I turn," he said, "you."

And here is desire based on pure aesthetics of the face: dark brows and lashes, strong nostrils, thick lips that pucker just so, and surprising dimples that come through when he talks. I couldn't get enough of him. I joined committees to be near. "Where I turn," he said, and I'd excuse myself. I'd justify my closeness. I contemplated sexual harassment charges.

His beard ended up on my phone as I surreptitiously took pictures of him during meetings, at the coffee shop downstairs as he sipped his Americano and me my cappuccino, as I fantasized our future together, an entire family. "Sister," he said as he walked by me and as I playacted typing in text to someone not here, "always there."

"Coincidences," I said.

At a company-wide meeting on productivity and morale, I sat behind him. I listened to managers and employees babble on about better years ago and better years to come when my purse tumbled from my lap to the floor. Still sitting, I reached down to get it. I smelled him, took in the tenor of his being, and needed to touch him. I sat up slowly and noted the dreadlocks. I could touch one of those, I thought, and he would never know. He may feel me do it, sure, but he wouldn't know that I did it purposely. When the convocation was over and we all stood, I reached up and touched one dreadlock. He moved away, forward, to leave the auditorium. The lock pulled between us and broke off where the hair had thinned from twisting. Of course he felt it.

When he turned, he saw me standing there with his hair in my hand, held like a stem of a flower without its bloom. "Wherever I turn. And what is that you have? My hair?"

"I'm so sorry."

"Doing some voodoo on me or something?"

"No, nothing like that."

He laughed at me. "I wasn't serious. You act as if you know something about it."

"Voodoo? I do. I have a friend."

His face grew serious. "Really? Now that's some Black folklore I wouldn't mind hearing about. Say, can I get my hair back?"

I handed him the lock. "I'm really sorry."

"No worries. I knew it was coming off, just didn't know when or where. It happens all the time. Not all the time, or I would be bald."

He plucked the hair from my hand. I felt the wooliness of it as it slid through my fingers. I closed my eyes and thought of heroines in movies, kissed finally. Instead, he said, "You're weird, you know, but next time we run into each other at the coffee shop, why don't we share a table? I want to know about voodoo."

I nodded at him and said sure. "What is your name?" I asked.

"Winter," he said and left, taking his dead dreadlock away with him.

French Fry Soup

On Tuesday nights they had French fry soup with the Jeffersons. The Jeffersons would wear matching T-shirts with some witty saying, and this ritual annoyed the Abduls, but they would never say as much to the Jeffersons. Tony Jefferson would point at his own chest when they arrived and say what was written on his shirt. "'It's five o'clock somewhere,' huh?" He'd repeat *huh* after saying something he considered witty. Amir Abdul didn't think Tony knew what wit was.

Amir hated that his first name began with the same letter as his last name. He felt like a children's book character when introducing himself. He always wanted to add, "And I love apples" whenever he told someone his name. "My name is Amir Abdul. And I love apples."

Amir's wife, Susan, hated apples and all fruit. She kind of liked bananas and would tolerate pears but only pears baked with bacon bits. She was disappointed to learn that Amir didn't eat bacon when they started dating. He used to think her ignorance endearing, but now he hated it. He wondered if his wife feigned stupidity to remain, what? cute? He wasn't sure.

Tony Jefferson married a big Black woman with doe eyes. "I had the name," he said, "so I had to find my Weezy." Amir couldn't help it: when Tony would point out the saying on his shirt, Amir would let his eyes wander to Weezy's shirt and look at the words stretched across her chest. "My other shirt is a Gucci," the shirt of that Tuesday read. The top of the G was lost on the underside of her right breast. He was determined to one day—hopefully soon—touch Weezy's breasts. He imagined her waiting there, in the kitchen, turned slightly away from the French fry soup bubbling away on the burner, turned toward him, and his two hands reaching like dependency toward her breasts.

French fry soup was a ridiculous thing, and French fry soup night was a sad occasion. If any one of them, anyone besides Amir, considered the pitifulness of collecting hard and uneaten French fries throughout the week only to be thrown in a pot with various vegetables and a broth reminiscent of chicken pot pie, they wouldn't do it anymore. Maybe instead, they'd go to that nice Ethiopian restaurant nearby or to some place Greek. He could enjoy a nice moussaka.

Amir could smell the potatoes flavor melding with all of the other veggies. He anticipated the soup being done. He watched Weezy as she got up to check it, watched her meaty hand ball itself into a fist and push against the arm of the chair as she rose, watched the flesh shift beneath the too-tight novelty tee. He stood up and followed her. His own wife, Susan, hated vegetables. She seemed a carnivore wholly, and she also liked her carbs: cake and cookies, rich breads, pie crusts. She remained thin, though, as if the beef and chicken and fatty sweets she consumed could not satiate nor sustain her figure.

Weezy, on the other hand, seemed to love all food. Amir sometimes would study Weezy eating and admire her careful little bites,
her plump lips blowing the soup cool on her spoon. He simply
wanted Weezy. He simply was coveting his neighbor's wife. And
now he couldn't contain the wait for her. He followed her into her
kitchen, thinking of her ripping pieces of bread apart so that she
could seamlessly gulp them up with hardly any notice. He would
watch her plop a square of toasty rye into the potato soup. So
now he followed her. "I will help you," he said, meaning to grab her
breasts when they were alone.

But he did not grab her breasts. He now felt the sadness for her
too. He felt awful that she had to make this soup base every Tuesday
for the Abduls to come over. He knew that years ago, she had had
a miscarriage. He knew that the daughter she did give birth to, the
one who survived the pregnancy, didn't call home often enough and
that her son could only call collect from jail. Touching her breasts
would make her less important than what she was, and she wasn't
important at all.

"I never like the T-shirts," he said.

Something in her was nervous. She moved as if among strangers. But she said, "They make Tony happy." She looked at Amir. "I
don't like them either."

Amir felt conspiratorial yet comfortable. He grinned at Weezy,
whose name was actually Allison. Were they now best friends?
Allison, Amir, Abdul, apples. How do you like those apples, Allison?
Amir thought.

Good Fit

Samana's legs were too long. Or the skirt was too short. She really could not settle on how the skirt was wrong. And her ass was too wide. In some circles it would be considered wide enough (or even not wide enough), but for her new job, was it too wide? She imagined, four months from now, the written evaluations from her students, 87 percent of whom would be white: "Her clothes were too provocative," "She was too urban," "She dressed nicely," "She looked unprofessional." If there was a question, Samana reasoned, if there was a concern, then the skirt wasn't right. And the shirt was too bright against her burnt umber skin. She took off the pink blouse and threw it on her bed. "Clothes aren't made for Black women," she thought.

She finally picked clothes that she considered professional but incognito, then made her way to the university. She was still awed that she got the job. A tenure-track position teaching writing at a university. First in her immediate family to get a college degree, first in her entire family to get an advanced degree, and she had, somehow, made it. Of course, the position was hundreds of miles from anyone she loved. And her new city was bereft of people who looked like her. But it was a job. A career in academia!

Once on campus, Samana tried to find her office with the map in her hiring packet. She had been to the campus twice before, but her sense of direction was horrible, and she had forgotten where everything was. Besides, the university was sprawled over one thousand acres, so finding any building wasn't easy. She disembarked from the bus near Adams Hall, so she wasn't too worried about getting lost. Still, she feared that she looked like a tourist and that someone would stop and offer help. And sure enough, an older gentleman wearing a bow tie and a tweed sportscoat came to her aid. "Do you need help finding one of your classes, Miss?" he said. "You still have a half an hour before the first sessions of the day."

Samana thought of the many responses she could offer her colleague, including "Black don't crack but I'm obviously not eighteen" or "Actually, sir, I was on my way to Chicago and I thought I'd stop here at this quaint little college in this quaint little town." But she smiled; his offer, she decided, was sincere, and she shouldn't be so suspicious. She introduced herself. "I'm Samana Towns. I'm joining the English Department this semester, and I can't remember where Adams Hall is."

"John Newton," the man shook her hand. "Welcome to campus! I have some time, so I can escort you, if you like. There are some good people in Adams. I'm over in Calvin Hall, myself, in chemistry." He led Samana to her building, which was only about a block away.

She went upstairs to her office and unlocked it, happy that she had moved most of her things in and placed the books on the shelves. Samana wanted to use the time before her class began to finish setting up her office. But should she leave her door opened or closed? If she kept it closed, she thought, then she may seem standoffish or uncooperative to her colleagues. Opened, then she may seem inconsiderate and brash depending on the noise. Samana stood at the threshold, holding the door ajar, trying to decide what she should do, when another colleague came to offer his help.

"Are you waiting for Dr. Towns?" he asked. "She should be in later this morning."

Samana looked at the man who stood there, jeans and plaid shirt, holding a coffee mug decorated with Shakespearean insults.

"Excuse me?" she said. "George, you interviewed me. I am Dr. Towns!"

"Oh." His face went immediately red. "It's just that you looked, uh—"

Samana waited, wanting him to complete the sentence because she was curious. But she wanted to fit in and not make her colleague uncomfortable, so she helped him out. "Lost, yes, I look lost. I was trying to decide if I wanted the door opened or shut."

George smiled. "We have an open-door culture here. Welcome, Samana! I'm so sorry."

She smiled back at him and nodded her head. "It's okay."

Her first class was two buildings away. She walked there, she worried, with the confidence of a first-year student—unsure of her surroundings or of the people. She found the building without issue and easily found her classroom. Students stood outside—her students—waiting for the class before theirs to end. One woman turned to Samana and looked her up and down. She was tall and blonde with fancy glasses and a flowery summer dress. She smiled and said hello, and Samana greeted her back. Then the student said, "I hope this Dr. Towns is not a dud. They're new, so no info on Rate My Prof."

Surely, there were nontraditional students on the campus, but didn't Dr. Towns at least look professorial to her student?

Apparently not. Samana started to correct her but decided instead to shrug. "We'll see," she said instead.

Soon the other class finished, so Samana and her students filed in. The young woman who had spoken to Samana in the hall tried to follow her, maybe meaning to sit next to her, but changed directions when she saw Samana stop at the head of the classroom and place her briefcase on the table. Eventually, the students found seats, and Samana looked out at them warmly. She looked forgivingly at the girl who had mistaken her for a student. She didn't want to make any of her students feel ashamed for making a faux pas on the first day of class, even though she was bothered by the girl.

Samana quickly introduced herself. She said they would begin with an icebreaker game. "Each person has to say their name and their major, then the next person has to say the previous student's name. The third student has to say the first two students' names, and so on, naming as many of the students before them as possible."

One of her male students raised his hand and said, "Don't you mean 'his or her' and not 'their' name? I mean, you're only talking about one person at a time, right?"

The question—the correction—almost caught Samana off guard. Wasn't this the generation that fought for the recognition of all genders? Beyond that, what was the student trying to prove by questioning his English professor's language? Still, keeping her decorum, Samana tried not to glare at the student for correcting her.

"I'm striving for inclusivity here," she said. "Not all of us may identify along the binary."

The student didn't respond but only gave her a hurt look.

"This is not high school," another young man said. "Why are we doing this name game?"

Samana's breath caught in her throat, and she coughed a little before answering. She did not expect these kinds of challenges on day one.

"This is a workshop where we'll be looking closely at each other's personal essays. You will very much want to know the people who are in this classroom. At the very least, you'll want to know their names."

Another man raised his hand. "I don't understand. Aren't all peer reviews online?"

Samana placed her fingertips on top of the table. "How's that now? Online?"

"Yes," he said, "all of the classes prior to this point—in English and otherwise—have peer reviews online."

"Who am I addressing, sir?"

"My name? I'm Ranger."

"Ranger," Samana said. "Huh. Well, this is a writing workshop where we'll parse through each other's pieces as a working group. But I am getting ahead of myself. I hope it suffices you to just understand that we need to know each other's names. We need to know each other. By the third week of this class, I want us to know each other more than—again, I am getting ahead. You first. Your name and major."

The class stumbled through the icebreaker, showing some mirth and cooperation. When they were all done, Samana told them her full name but asked that they address her as Professor Towns. A student named Emily asked what was the meaning of the name Samana.

"It's the name of the town where my great-grandfather was born and raised. It's in the DR."

"So then you're not American?" Ranger asked.

"My great-grandfather was from Samaná, but he immigrated to the States for work and fell in love with my great-grandmother."

Rosalie, the same girl who had talked to her in the hallway about the professor being a potential dud, raised her hand. "Have you even published anything before? No offense, but you look so young."

"Not only that," one of the men whose name she couldn't remember said, "it's that, you know, are you a diversity hire?"

"A what?" Samana asked.

"No offense, but there aren't many colored faculty—"

"You mean faculty of color—"

"Right, there aren't that many here, so ...," the student trailed off.

"So you think I was only hired because of my race." Samana watched the student start to speak, then stop himself. She glanced around at the rest of the class. Each white face looked guilty. "Should I open the question up to everyone?"

"Do you want to be here?" someone asked.

"Of course!"

"But you're not from here," someone else said.

"She's not American," Ranger said.

"I am American." Could her class see that she was so angry that her ears were red? They probably could not. They might not have known to look. "Did anyone bother to look me up online? I thought everyone Googled their professors."

"There's Rate My Professor."

"No, find out about your professors. Learn about their research, their publications, their credentials. Learn where they got their degrees."

"Where did you get your degree?"

Samana took a breath and sat down. "Do you know how academia works? Do any of you know how I got this job?"

The students shook their heads. "It's just that you're so young," one student said, "so you could not possibly be a doctor, right?"

"I'm not that young." Samana could do two things, and she knew this: she could get angry, or she could treat this as a teaching moment. She decided to do both.

"Let's talk a little about the academic job market and how it works. Before I begin, I just want you to know that you need an advanced degree to teach here unless you're a TA, and I am not a TA. And in the English Department, you need a PhD."

Samana then told the students about how faculty jobs are advertised and how few jobs there were. She told them that her position was coveted, and though race may have been an asset to her employment ("I will never know. No one will ever tell me if I was hired to make the rainbow more complete," she told them), it was not enough to secure her the position.

"So, have I published anything? Of course I have. You can learn about any of my publications if you do just a minute of research. But let's not talk about me, okay? Let's do some writing. I'll write a one-page bio, and you all will do the same. Type up anything you want the class to know about you and bring it with you the next time we meet. I'll bring mine too."

That night Samana cried to her mother, who was nearly one thousand miles away, who consoled her over the phone.

"You deserve to be there," her mother said. "You have the background and the degrees. You did the hard work that won you that spot."

"But I don't fit in. It's so important for faculty to be a good fit, Mama, and I'm not. That's apparent."

"Of course they want you to think that," her mother said. "Honey, remember when you first went to college? Your daddy and I drove you five hundred miles away and settled you in. When we got home, you had left us four voice messages telling us to come back."

"Mama, this is different."

"It's the same damn thing. You complained that there were no Black people, no people of color, no poor people. You complained that your roommate only listened to heavy metal."

"But that was for only four years."

"We had to leave you there for a month until you found friends."

"This is a career. This is my life! I can't live like this."

"A whole month until you found your friends, your favorite teachers, and comfort. You came home for a weekend, and you were happy to go back to school."

"You're telling me to give it a month?"

"You are a grown woman. Give it a year."

The next day wasn't as horrible for Samana. She had two students of color in her first-year composition course and met another professor of color, a gender studies professor who was Southeast Asian. She even had lunch with George, who again apologized for not recognizing her.

"It's just that you look like a student or something," he said.

She considered just accepting his apology but decided instead to dig at her soreness. "George," she began, "was it like this for you when you first started here?"

"What do you mean?"

Samana took a sip of her latte. She continued. "You're, what, in your thirties? Early forties?"

"Late thirties." He bit his sandwich, and while still chewing, he said, "But I'm just a pasty white guy. And you have good skin."

"Oh? But I don't look like a kid, right? I'm not saying that our students are kids; they're young adults. But they are so much younger than me. And I know there are nontraditional students here, but they look, I don't know." Samana stopped speaking. "I don't know how to say this."

"You're hurt that I mistook you for a student?"

"Yes, I am."

"But you should feel like it's a compliment. You do look pretty young."

"George, we've met. You interviewed me. You escorted me from the airport when I was here for my campus visit. I know I should feel flattered that people—and yes, it's many people here on campus—mistake me for a student, but really, I feel like it challenges my professionalism. Is it the way I dress? Or is it the skin?"

"The good skin."

"Mmm," Unsatisfied with his response, Samana let the argument go. She smiled at George. "I hope I didn't make you feel uncomfortable."

"Me? Samana, you're the one who should be uncomfortable. You think it's a race thing?"

Samana nodded and laughed. "Oh, yeah, I do." George looked worried. "See? You're uncomfortable." Samana laughed again.

On the third day of classes, she met her nonfiction class again, and they dutifully brought in their bios. She learned that they were high school valedictorians, prom and homecoming queens, and star quarterbacks. Her students were late bloomers or early readers, guitarists, flutists, drummers, and violinists. Her students had published in the student literary journal and student newspaper. They hoped for the annihilation of entire countries or world peace. They had cats; they had dogs, guinea pigs and hamsters, snakes, fish, and even a miniature pony. They listened to rap, pop, country, and hip-hop.

Her students were also sometimes hungry, sometimes homeless, and sometimes defiant. They had family they had to take care of; they had two jobs so they could afford tuition; they had to put things off.

"Where's Ranger?" Samana asked.

Her students shrugged. She was disappointed that he was not there. She wanted to show him—she wanted to show them all—that she had a right to be there and that she was the best choice. Samana shrugged herself, sad that she may have lost one but grateful that most of her students had stayed.

After class Rosalie went to Samana at the front of the classroom. "I think our prof is not a dud. Well, not so far," she said.

Samana grinned at her. "Good! It's probably because she has a class full of bright and talented students."

"Will you ever tell us how old you are?"

"Rosalie, as a writer, we learn how to figure that out without asking. I'm sure you can search for me online and find my age if you want to. Maybe we will discuss fact-finding in class."

After Rosalie left, Samana thought about what her mother had told her over the phone the other night: she deserved to be there. She had done the work to land her the position at that midwestern university. Samana agreed, but that she had earned a spot there did not change the way people treated her. She felt as if she were borrowing space and time until someone more worthy came along. She could call her mother and complain again, after her first week of school, ask for advice. But, Samana thought, if she considered herself fit for the part, she had better stop indulging in expectations and challenging all assumptions.

Samana gathered her book bag and left the classroom. The hallways of the building in which she taught were now familiar to her and were starting to feel like a home at work. It helped that her office was there, too, full of books and objects she had collected over the years. Outside of Adams Hall, she nodded and greeted the people she passed by, as is custom in that midwestern state. One of the people was Ranger, who smirked instead of smiled. He nodded once, cowboy fashion, and said, "Professor," the greeting full of sarcasm.

"So sorry you had to drop my class."

"Wasn't a match for my schedule."

As they exchanged hooded pleasantries, they both kept walking, going in their respective directions. That kid did not like Samana, and she was pretty sure the feeling was mutual. How many Rangers would she have during her time at that university, she wondered. However many, she had better get used to it; she couldn't possibly please everyone or convince them of her worth.

As she left the institutional beauty of the campus's lawns and buildings, she felt herself become more buoyant. She had finished her first week of school. She was getting to know her students and colleagues, and she knew that her position at the university was just as meritorious as that of any of the other professors. How could she doubt herself? She was perfect for the job, and she would move her campus forward. Of course she was a good fit.

PART VI

I have heard, but not believ'd,
the spirits o' th' dead
May walk again.

—WILLIAM SHAKESPEARE,
The Winter's Tale

We All Have Our Ghosts

We all have our ghosts, but we mostly ignore them as our conscious or quiet thoughts. They only bother us when they say things we don't want to hear. Only then do we perk up and listen. Don't think this is a kind of psychosis or illness. These aren't voices in our head. They are voices of those about us, not whispering but talking. Sometimes yelling. When they come, you could pay attention, or you could go away.

Twice before, ghosts came to me and I knew exactly who they were. The first ghost was my grandmother. She was lying in state in her parlor, of course in her best clothes—her high holiday church clothes—her hair made up fresh by a beautician who somehow got the job of dolling up the dead. I got tired of welcoming people to the end of her life, so I dipped out to get air. Grandmother, twenty years younger than the day she died and still shapely, stood on the porch. She kept her shape most of her life. "You can smoke," she said. She lit a cigarette and inhaled. "It's so sweet to smoke again." I closed my eyes and told her that I loved her. Maybe she reached out and touched my shoulder? I don't know. I opened my eyes, and she was gone.

I could do that. I could close my eyes and breathe like I'm doing yoga. The ghost will note that you don't want to talk to them, then leave. I did it with my grandmother, and I've done it with Bill, my first boyfriend in college, who shot himself either accidentally or on purpose. The first time I saw Bill, I screamed. His brains perpetually seeped from a textured hole in his head. I screamed loudly, and my roommate, who is now dead herself, came in and asked if I was okay. "It's Bill," I said.

"I know," she said. "I'm sorry."

"No," I said. "He is here."

"Here."

"I see him."

"Close your eyes," she said. I did. Breathed with her, in for one-two-three-four-five and held, two-three, and out, four-three-two-one. We breathed like that three or four times more, our fingertips touching, and the world steadied. I opened my eyes, and Bill was gone.

Two days later, Bill was back. He sat at my desk, like he used to do, eating an apple. This time his head was whole. "Do you taste the apple?" I asked him.

He nodded. "It's sweet."

I nodded back at him. "Was it an accident?" He took another bite of his apple and chewed thoughtfully. I thought: bovine. Ruminating. He was kind of round, and I used to like grabbing the folds of his belly and squeezing him lightly. We never really broke up.

"That's why I wanted to come back," he said. "I mean, there are no mistakes, right? No accidents like that, anyway. But I don't think I consciously wanted to do it."

"It just happened?" I asked.

"It just happened."

But Bill and my grandmother, those aren't the ghosts who are always talking. I don't know the talking ghosts. They say useless things. For instance, one tells me the last conversation she had with her husband was a fight. Maybe a fight that got too heated. Others tell me to watch for cars or not to watch for cars. They tell me the secret properties of cats and that I should have at least one pet cat. They tell me whether to pick the peach or the orange sherbet. I never see them. I don't know why. Maybe it's because I wouldn't have recognized them. Maybe it's because they don't need to be seen. But I can't close my eyes against them, and they can't go away. I can quiet them by doing the breathing, but I can still hear the tone of their voices humming in the background of the living, sounding like faraway radio music.

A third ghost visits me now. I can see her. At first I'm not sure who she is, and her presence is unsettling. She is haunting me. The others were just there. Grandmother and Billy just wanted to tell me one thing: Grandmother that she was okay and Billy that it wasn't me that made him do it. Maybe not me. He was confused when he was alive, and he is confused now that he's dead. "Maybe you never actually saw him," my roommate told me when she was still here. "Maybe it's just your consciousness telling you not to blame yourself, that it wasn't your fault that he—" but she didn't finish her sentence. She holds her breath. What would she have said? Offed himself? Stupidly shot himself in the temple? Or was it the forehead? I don't know. I never want to know. His casket was closed, of course.

This third ghost used to go away. I'd breathe in, hold, then breathe out, and poof: she'd disappear. When my curiosity gets to me, I ask her why she is here. She opens her mouth and says nothing. Only holds her mouth open. Then opens it wider. Her tongue is bruise-colored purple, and her teeth, though yellowed and cracked, hang on tenaciously to her gums. Then she closes her mouth, and that somehow frightens me more. I close my eyes and count. Hold my breath and breathe out. I open my eyes, and she is still there but shimmery, wavering like a migraine.

I should recognize her. I think I do not because I refuse to believe she would haunt me.

Once I tell her I don't want her here. "I am not sure who you are, and I don't know how to help you. You won't talk to me." I do the yoga thing, and when I open my eyes, she is staring at me with her mouth agape. She scratches lazily at one of her breasts. The cloth of her well-worn peasant blouse tears easily at her fingernails. Skin from her chest rubs away. I leave the room, and she doesn't follow me.

I don't see her again for days and think I'm free. I think of her as a waking nightmare. Then I see the ghost of my roommate. She is in my bedroom sitting on my bed as I get ready to leave, as she often did when she was alive. My roommate's ghost looks over my shoulder as I twist my hair into a goddess crown, do my eye makeup, put on my foundation and lipstick. I talk to her, and I see her mouth fall open in a state of comfort, of listening. She wheezes lightly as she did often when alive. I look away, back to myself in the mirror, then back to my roommate, whose mouth is still open. Spittle the color of red rust on the edges of sharp things spills from the side of her lip. My stomach drops. "Are you okay?" I ask her. She closes her mouth, and I get a chill all over.

A talking ghost convinces me to get an Americano instead of my regular cappuccino. She keeps telling me how nice my hair is. Another ghost comes in and tells me that he'll help me study for my test. I don't know where they are physically, but I sit at a two-person booth alone. The girl ghost tells me what to eat at coffee shops. "I was a barista," she says. "I'm telling you how to get the best drinks—cheap and healthier—for your money."

The other ghost says, "Why don't you take your math book out?" so I do, hoping that he is better at Calculus II than me, praying that he took it. I open the book to chapter 4. "Ah," he says, "this is all coming back to me. Quickly now."

"You keep forgetting she died in pain," the girl ghost says.

"Do I?" I say. I hope I am quiet. I hope I whisper-mumbled this to myself. Very quietly, mostly in my head, I say, "I do keep forgetting," remembering again that my roommate was found dead. Or I didn't want to remember. And when she visited me as a ghost, I think I wanted so much for her to be at peace that I ignored what I knew.

The haunting ghost shows up then. My roommate. How could I recognize her in that state, though? Like Billy's, her casket was closed too. And she was cremated and carried home by her grieving parents. Now, slowly, she opens her mouth, and I understand everything. The chocolate her boyfriend fed her whenever he promised to be good to her from that point forward. The raspy-ness of her breathing. "Do you blame me for repressing it?" I ask.

She shakes her head no.

The talking ghost says, "She wants you to kill him. It's the only way that she'll go away."

I cover my ears and close my eyes. I breathe in for five counts, hold for three counts, and breathe out. When I open my eyes again, the talking ghosts are muted, their voices too soft to hear. My roommate is still there, though. She stares at me with her open mouth and the rust-colored drool dripping from her lips. I don't flinch away or close my eyes; I look at her and search for the laugh lines that were coming in early because, as everyone knew, she laughed so much. "I didn't know that he hurt you physically. And the chocolate. Not until you told me later. I didn't know he was the one who did this."

What could she have told me? That it was only this one time? That it was an accident? A game? Could she have told me that she had suffered with him for the two years they were together but still, hopelessly, she agreed to marry him? I was going to be one of her bridesmaids. I should have known. "I should have," I say, "but I didn't."

The next day I find myself in her boyfriend's neighborhood. I know where he lives; I dropped her off at his house many times. I picked her up from there. Sometimes she would be sitting on the stoop, looking smaller than her actual size. Did I know then? I don't think I did—but the truth of what I was aware of harried me.

The area is familiar to me, as is the duplex where he lives and the car in the driveway—a souped-up Dodge Daytona with a ridiculously large spoiler and an iridescent paint job. I slow as I pass the bungalow, expecting to see him inside. Doing what? Cooking something? Watching television?

Later I'm in bed when my roommate comes to me again. She is wearing her favorite pajamas, the footed ones. It is summer now, warm and muggy, but the pajamas seem right. It is her normal roommate visit; that is, this is how her ghost looks when she isn't suffering. "You want me to kill him," I say.

She says: "You realize when you can't breathe how precious breathing is. When you hold your breath for those ten counts or more, when you are not allowed to take in oxygen, what keeps you going is the anticipation of that next breath. And the one after that. What makes holding your breath so effective is the understanding that you will be rewarded with countless breaths after that. A lifetime of breathing.

"I saw before I realized that I was no longer allowed breath. First, just the inside of my lids and the light from the sun playing on them. I waited for the ability to taste air again. But it didn't come. And then there were varicolored pinpricks that turned to stars. Those turned to sheaths of color like a broadly painted rainbow. Then there was nothing at all. A silence that wasn't silence. A darkness that wasn't darkness. I didn't even know enough to know that I wouldn't breathe again. An ignorance without knowledge, if that makes sense. There was nothing."

My stomach tickles like I will be sick, but instead of throwing up, I cry. My roommate's smile is light on her face, as if she is listening to me. I can see the little lines playing at the corner of her eyes, along the distance from her nose to the edges of her mouth, at the edges of her lips. Then she fades away.

Why would it not be easy to get into his house? The only obstacle I have is not an obstacle. It is all the ghosts. Some cheering me on. Fewer trying to stop me. One asking over and over again, "What can vengeance give you but more pain?" And when I park my car three blocks away, when I shut my engine, the anti-vengeance ghost says, "He will become a ghost too." That almost stops me, but I carry on. I walk to his bungalow. I'm wearing satin gloves though it is over eighty degrees. I ring his doorbell, and he is there. He answers.

His expression, when he sees me, is a mixture of surprise and expectation. He hardly hesitates before moving aside and letting me in. When he closes the door behind me, he hugs me, and I hug him back. What is unnerving is the lack of things happening in my roommate's boyfriend's house. The television isn't on. The radio or stereo isn't on. His laptop isn't open. There is no evidence of a book or anything. What was he doing before I arrived? It feels like he was waiting for me.

"I miss her so much," he says.

"I do too."

"Would you like something to drink? Please have a seat."

I sit down and look around me. His apartment is orderly and unremarkable. "I've never been here before," I say.

"Would you like a drink?"

"No."

He sits down across from me. "Did you want to talk?"

I nod. "I suppose that's why I've come. I've been thinking about her a lot." He nods, so I continue. "And I've been thinking about how we both lost someone. It's—" I stop. Where am I going with this? Her ghost is here, as sudden as a breeze on a still day. She whispers in my ear: strange. "It's strange," I said. "I'm not feeling lonely, though."

"No?"

"No. What were you doing when I got here?"

"Huh?"

"Before I rang your bell? What were you doing?"

He shrugs. "She used to ask me that. Sometimes, when I get home for work, I just sit on the floor and meditate. That's what I was doing. Sitting on the floor and following thoughts."

My roommate whispers: he's only telling part of the truth. You will never know the entire truth.

"I don't miss her that much," I say, "because I feel like—this is going to sound mad."

"No," he says. "Go ahead."

"I talk to her. All the time. She tells me—"

He sits up. His face flinches. He thinks I'm mad. "Tells you what?"

"That your relationship was more than what it seemed. She told me that you hurt her. You did, right?"

"Hurt her?" He shrugs again. "We argued. We argued like any couple." He stands up. "Would you like something to drink?"

Roommate whispers: this is the part of the truth he wants you to know. "Please, sit down. I don't want a drink."

He walks over and sits next to me. "It felt good to hug you," he says. "The funeral and immediately after the funeral, everyone was there for me. And then everyone was gone. I didn't want to hassle anyone with my wants. I didn't call for help. I felt alone." He tears up, and something in my stomach shifts.

Roommate says: he is not lying, but he is not telling the entire truth. "The cops," he says, "came around many times and asked about our fights. Sometimes there were fights. She threw things, I said things, and sure, I hit her once or twice, but not, you see, I never wanted to really hurt her. I just wanted to stop her." He pulls the collar down on his shirt. "But she meant to scar me." He shows me a discolored bit of skin carved into his chest right beneath his collarbone. "This is from her fingernail file." He pulls his collar down lower, unbuttoning a little to show me more. "These are her teeth marks."

"But why?" I ask.

He looked at me like I was slow in catching on. "You're seeing her ghost," he says. I want to correct him and tell him that no, I'm seeing her ghosts, that I'm seeing so much of her, so many manifestations of my roommate. He takes me in his arms and holds me close. I feel the naked parts of his chest against me. "Her ghost tells you that I hurt her." I don't say anything. He rubs my back, and I let him. He nuzzles his nose into my neck, and I let him. He moves a hand down my spine to my behind. He traces the band of my pants and moves his hand around to the front of me. He pushes me back gently, unbuttons my pants, and I let him. He rubs the outside of my panties, and I gasp even though I don't want to. My roommate whispers: keep going. Let him. I let him get comfortable, but I get comfortable too. There are pillows all around us, and I've kept my gloves on.

Soon we're both nearly naked. The excitement of being touched again after I lost my boyfriend and the thrill of what I am about to do arouse me, move me to climax before anything has begun. He gets excited, too, of course, and he takes down his pants, his boxers.

He has his penis in his hand, and I worry that he will come on me. I don't want a mess. I don't want a trace. I grab a throw pillow and cover his face. With my entire weight, I bear down on him. We tumble from the couch to the floor. I still have the pillow against his face. He struggles beneath me. I worry that my hairs, my skin, will rub off onto his body. But I have to finish.

"I have my ghosts, and surely, you do too," I tell him. I lift the pillow from his face, and he gasps for air. When he breathes out, he cries "Bitch" at me, and I put the pillow down. I count slowly. One. Two. Three. Four. Five.

I lift the pillow. "Do you see her? Does she visit you in your dreams?"

I am sitting on his hands, and he tries to scratch my butt. I try to squeeze his scrotum flat with my thighs. He is stronger than me, and he doesn't believe he is going to die. I let him wriggle his hands free only so that I can get them beneath my knees. We wrestle more, and I keep my voice low. He calls me bitch many times over. Finally, I get his wrists beneath me. I slam down with my knees, hoping it's hard enough to break his wrists. At any rate he screams when we connect, and I cover his face again with the throw pillow. I count.

The few times I lift the pillow—to rest, to see if it's working, to give him space to apologize—I see how his face changes from a living man who walks around this earth with choices, with decisions to make, with likes and dislikes. I see in his eyes that he once knew death would eventually come but that it was not imminent for him. He has no worry of dying, no fear. I see that change into a man facing every action he took in the past, those decisions he did make, including with my roommate. I see in him defeat, sorrow for losing his own life but not regret for the life he led. I see in him the ghost that he will become, and I tell him that I will never see him. I promise him that.

I lift the pillow one more time when I know that he has finally succumbed to death. He looks almost peaceful. His mouth closed. His nose bleeding just a little. He stares beyond my shoulder. Maybe he sees her. I could stop there and let him live, but I see that man is still there. The man who killed at least one woman and who would never feel culpable. So, to be sure, I cover his face one final time until I am certain his breathing has ceased.

I walk away from him and away from ghosts for good. I am not naive; I know the ghosts will still try to come, but I will fill my world with noises so I won't hear them whispering or see the ones who don't want to go away.

Minutes later, in my car, I see him once more. He appears with a blue face and sleepy eyes. "I made you feel good, right?" his ghost says. "Before you acted. Did it feel good to kill me too?"

"Yes, it did."

"Will you kill again?"

I close my eyes against him. When I open them again, his ghost is gone.

Dancing Queen

The seer looked into her disco ball of lives, lies, likenesses, and possibilities. Her heavily eye-lined and mascaraed eyes peered back at her. Squares of light from the illuminated ball dotted her face. On her hand was a tattoo of the Eye of Isis. Her breath smelled like decades' worth of cigarette smoke. She smiled slightly but more than the Mona Lisa. Three of her teeth were missing. One tooth blackened and one tooth covered in gold.

"Do you want to know what I want to know?" the seeker asked.

"What kind of fortune teller would that make me?" the seer asked.

The seeker waited. Faint chimes of ancient bells played on the air.

The fortune teller murmured, burped, excused herself, and cleared her throat. "You will dance tonight," she said. "Don't go home when you think it's time. Wait until you smell jasmine."

The seeker stood up. "That it?"

The fortune teller looked up at the woman. She nodded. "But there's always more." She smiled again. "And you don't want more."

"How much?"

"I can only ask for a donation."

The seeker dug in her purse and gave some amount of money. She left the tent in tears, remembering the last time she danced.

All the Dreams You've Yet to Have

Kaizah searched for something worth saving. In the past her family sewed quilts from remnants of cloth or from old clothes worn ragged. Her great-grandmother's house was once a slave barracks, then a sharecropper's home, and it grew from the remnants of the abandoned shacks beside it, from dilapidated wooden tools, from splinters of fallen trees. Kaizah's mother and father's knowledge came from a patchwork of horse sense, family legends, street smarts, and an American school education.

The leftovers, the scraps, the bits people discard.

Bene's clothes were still in the closet. His shoes: on the rack by the front door. His work boots: by the back door. In his shaver behind the head, some of his chin hairs and one dreadlock she had cut from his head. The food that he ate—the chicken bone from the last meal he shared with Kaizah—was still there. Kaizah froze it along with the fried corn and the collards he was about to eat ("Saving that for last," he said) before he died.

Kaizah wanted Bene back. She knew people who could help,

including her sister and mother, but she couldn't bring herself to go to anyone in her family. Instead, she went to a shop on the pretense of getting her fortune read. Inside there was a white woman dressed in a colorful *lehenga*, a peasant blouse, and a shawl made of batik. The cultures clashing on the woman was enough to make Kaizah want to go away, but she stayed to see. "You the only one here?" Kaizah said.

"You think I'm not good enough?"

"I think you're confused."

"You came to get your fortune read, so sit down and let me read it. Don't be prejudiced."

Kaizah sat where the woman pointed. "Black people can't be prejudiced," she said.

The woman ignored the remark and sat across from Kaizah. "I'm Diamond, by the way."

"That's your Christian name?"

"I ain't a Christian." At first she did nothing but stare at Kaizah. Her scrutiny was so raw that Kaizah felt as if the woman was physically touching her. "You are obviously in pain," Diamond said. "Hey, give me your hands."

When Diamond took her hands, Kaizah could feel the coolness of the gold and silver on Diamond's fingers. Her hands, too, were cool, and Kaizah was impressed; the woman was making herself neutral.

"Someone died," Diamond said. "I ain't trying to be a psychic; it's just that obvious. A lover?"

"A husband."

"You don't want to see me. You came to see her."

"Who's her?"

"I can tell that you have something in your bag for her. This doesn't feel right; I think you should leave."

"If there is a *her*, let her tell me to leave."

Another woman appeared in the rear of the store. She was Black. A small, ancient woman wearing sweatpants and a T-shirt that was probably two sizes too big for her. "Let the woman figure it out when she get the facts," the old Black woman said.

Annoyed, Diamond quickly gestured at the woman. "Madeline," she said and slightly bowed.

"This woman has experienced grief," Madeline said. "Anyone can see that; you're right about that, Diamond. She carries in her bag earthly things. But what she wants isn't exactly earthly. You have a past with this religion? You knew what to grab."

"I want to make a quilt," Kaizah said.

That night, as instructed, Kaizah laid Bene's things out on his side of the bed. She sprinkled the mixture Miss Madeline gave her over Bene's belongings and whispered the incantation she had acquired by rote. She closed the ceremony by saying: "Because I love you. Because I don't like being here without you." Then she went downstairs and waited. First on the couch. She tried to sleep but couldn't keep her eyes shut. Next with a cup of tea. She sipped so slowly, the tea went cold. Then with video games. She played without pleasure. When hours passed, when she had nearly forgotten what she was waiting for, Bene came.

His walk was the same, only slower and smaller. His broad shoulders had narrowed, and he held them curled into himself. He was diminutive, and that wasn't the case before.

And Bene had a new sound. His dreaded hair was rough as sandpaper, and she could hear the dreadlocks shifting together. His steps were soft but lifeless, fleshlike thuds against an ungiven surface. And Kaizah could hear a rattling in his chest or throat, like mucus drying and trying to break free.

But still, he was beautiful to Kaizah. He was the man she had fallen for. He was the one she had promised to love through good and bad times. She stood to greet him, and he stopped, just a few feet from her. His eyes were flatter; she could see that. The light in the greenish hazel of his eyes was gone, and they shone more brown than green. Still! "Bene," she said.

He opened his mouth. The rattle within him grew louder, and in spite of herself, Kaizah shivered.

He closed his mouth again. Speaking, at least for now, was too much. Kaizah went to her husband and held him. He opened his mouth, rattled again, and she hugged tighter. The sensation, she noted, was like holding empty garments. "You hungry, baby?"

Bene held her back by hugging her with stiff arms. Kaizah went cold. She had wanted this, she told herself. This was good. So, she and Bene held onto each other in their living room. Bene opened his mouth again and put it so close to Kaizah's ear, as he did in life—close enough to taste it, they used to say, so he sometimes would take a lick with his tongue, but not now. He opened his mouth again, and Kaizah heard flesh and skin pull apart. "I don't eat," Bene said.

"You don't eat," Kaizah said. Her heart was beating hard enough to shake them both. "Let's sit down, Bene. Come on, over to the couch." She gently pulled herself away from him. He followed her, but he didn't sit. Kaizah wondered if he could bend.

In college her philosophy professor said that no one has come back to tell us, so we depend on faith in God. Or we could not believe. But here, Kaizah thought, was a man who had come back. Would it be rude to ask him now, when he only so recently found life again and his voice? Also, she hoped he'd get better at talking soon; conversation is what Kaizah missed the most.

She could ask. He'd tell her, she was sure. He stood before her, waiting, smelling of fresh cut dahlias and lilies and something earthy. "Were you," she started but stopped herself. What if he had gone to hell, if there was an afterlife? Bene breathed in. His chest rattled.

She tried again, giving him the benefit of the doubt because Bene was a good man. "What was heaven like, Bene?"

Her husband looked at her, his eyes growing flatter. "I dreamed good dreams. I had good sleep. So restful."

"No harp?"

"I'm tired and want to sleep again."

"You're too young to sleep like that. You're up now."

Bene stayed dead. Kaizah was convinced that the spell Madeline gave her was created to taunt her. Or maybe it was a lesson spell, a conjuring to tell you to be careful what you ask for. Three weeks after Bene's resurrection, Kaizah noticed three problems she couldn't deal with. The first was the cleanliness, or the lack thereof. He'd do nothing but sit there all day with his flat eyes and rattling chest, and Kaizah would bathe him at night. Each night the bathwater would run mud brown. Sand and silt would cover the bottom of the tub.

The second thing was the lack of regeneration. His nails grew for that first week, then stopped. They were long and blackening. She tried not to think it, but the word worked itself into her mind: *rotting*. His hair was longer than it ever was when he was alive, but he'd lose dreadlocks quite often. They would fall off. She couldn't moisturize his hair no matter how hard she tried, so it stayed dry. She'd find dreads in areas all over the house, which bothered her because he didn't seem to move much. On his head were shiny bald patches where a dreadlock used to be.

Third, he slept a lot. Almost as much as a cat. He'd ask her to sleep with him, and she found out that it was not a euphemism; he wanted to sleep. Once they did try sex, but she couldn't perform with his flat eyes on her. And he wasn't interested. But he wanted to sleep all the time. "It's the best rest, Kaizah. If you just sleep with me."

Kaizah knew what he was asking. "Couldn't you get energy somehow?"

"I have suspicions of how, but neither of us would want that."

Kaizah took his hand and looked at him. "I suppose I have to see this life that I do have through."

"I can't be like this much longer."

Kaizah ran the bathwater and guided Bene up to the bath. She undressed him and helped him into the tub. The water almost immediately went from clear to brown, a color as rich as her own skin. "Does dying hurt?"

"I don't remember. I suppose it does, but eventually, it doesn't. And then it's every wonderful dream you've had. It's all the dreams you've yet to have."

"Ever have any nightmares?" Kaizah undressed herself.

"If your dreams start teetering into undesirable places, you veer yourself away from those territories. Eventually, you become lucid in those dreams, moving about as you would if you were awake."

She got into the bath with him, and he held her. His skin was neither warm nor cold. The texture was not unlike clay. They lay in the tub, holding each other, and Kaizah let herself drift off. She had a wonderful dream of being pregnant, her belly fat and round. She was wearing a yellow-and-white patterned dress. Bene was there, full of life. He smiled with his whole face. His teeth the impossible white they were, his gums pink, his dimples accenting his long face. They were laughing about something. It was the kind of sunny day that felt nostalgic, a summer day of memories. But she was never pregnant.

She woke up. She turned in the tub to look at her husband. "Do you ever wake up?"

"Not exactly," he said. "But you see how sweet that dream was?"

"Yes," she said. "I do." She ran the hot water again to let the tub heat up. She turned the tap off and let herself drift off.

L'autunno

We stripped to nothing and jumped into the calm lake. We were on the edge of young adulthood and certain that it was our final chance to behave recklessly before heading into responsibility.

The cool, pleasant water enveloped us when the surrounding New England woods grew quiet. "Did the tree frogs go to sleep?" one of us asked. We listened and heard stillness, a quietness such as before the hardest part of a storm.

Then Ann disappeared.

She sunk quickly, creating a weird *plunk!* noise. Then she was gone. Before we could look for her, Nate went under. Leonard dived after them and never came up.

Have you ever heard an underwater scream? We listened for it but heard nothing. Melody and I swam for shore. The tree frogs started in again, then the crickets. We climbed out of the water and looked back. Autumn-orange leaves dropped into the lake, covering every bit of blue until there was none. Carefully, I reached forward and touched the leaves where the water should have been but only felt earth beneath my fingers.

An Opossum Tale

"Do they eat cucumbers?" Ryan asked. He tried to scratch at the opossum's neck. She recoiled and hissed.

"Don't give him any cukes," Toni said. "Then he'd be coming in my garden all the time. I don't want that."

"She. It's a she."

"You an opossum expert now? Just a big, ugly rodent."

"It's a marsupial. One of the few marsupials in North America." Ryan reached at the animal again, and she hissed again. "I only know because I see her nipples. Preggo."

"Shit. Can't we move her? Would her ol' man be looking for her?"

"I don't know if they monogamous, you know? I tend to see them solo or the mama with her babies."

"Hanging off her like Christmas tree lights. I seen that before. At night they get red eyes. I seen that too. Can you move her, Ryan? I don't want her in my garden."

They were in her garden now, down around the cucumbers, tomatoes, and the marigolds that kept pests at bay. Magic socks, which were old socks filled with what Toni was told was animal deterrents, hung from a clothesline. Piano music softly played from outdoor speakers. "What's that you listening to?" Ryan asked.

"Not me, the plants. They like Baroque. This is Scarlatti. They like Bach and Corelli too."

"I forgot you knew all that white music. That and gospel."

"Can you move her, Ryan?"

He sat back on his haunches. He looked around at the garden, at the sunflowers starting to bloom and the squash filling out. "I need more than vegetables this time, Toni. You got any money?"

Toni tried to not sneer at Ryan, but she felt her lips turn up on the left side of her face. He knew she had money. She was all but retired, just working part-time. And although he didn't have to, Reverend Saunders paid her under the table for playing organ at the church. She was one of the few homeowners on her block. "I can write you a check if you show me the opossum."

Later that night Toni went over all her regrets: leaving her husband when she caught him cheating, not telling her daughter why she left her father, not fighting to see her grandkids, not remarrying though she had ample opportunity. Eventually, she'd be dead, and she'll leave everything to her daughter and grandkids, though they'd have nothing to do with her. For all they knew, she was just an old, bitter woman.

Her newest regret was falling in with Ryan's grandmother, a woman even older than Toni. When Toni went to her, she was surprised at how ancient the woman looked. Her wrinkles cut deep furrows in her skin, and the skin between was more gray than brown. An ancient woman. "You like things that ain't you," she had said to Toni. "Europe. You like Bach, Caravaggio, and all the Baroque era art. How come?"

"I don't think it's not me. Race is a social construct." Toni used to teach that when she was still teaching social studies at Malcom X

Academy. "Still," she had told her students, "racism can exist because that, too, is a construct." To Ryan's grandmother, who preferred the name Bunny, she said, "And I don't limit myself to dead white artists."

"Of course not. You like rap music too. That, too, ain't you. You lived a life that belonged to something else. What it is that you want?"

"Only for the animals to stay out of my garden."

"You say that, but that ain't all it. That's all you'll tell me." Then Bunny filled a satchel with various things and gave it to Toni for a fee. "Hang that up around your garden. Socks work as a vessel for most folk. The magic comes as an animal. If you take it away, you'll lose something dear."

Remember this conversation, it dawned on Toni: *the opossum is the animal.* She was protecting Toni's garden! Toni started up and wondered if she could stop Ryan, hoped that if he was going to trap her, he'd use a no-kill trap. She swooned with the thought of using magic, was sure that she was losing her mind in her old age. She rushed outside to find Ryan, drinking on her porch swing, dressed for bed. "I just want to see," he said, "how she living."

"Just leave her, Ryan."

"Are you scared of me?"

"No. I don't want to kill the possum."

"I still want my money."

"I have forty dollars. I'll give you that and a bag for vegetables. Just leave the possum."

Ryan chuckled and shook his head at her. "Batty as Bunny," he said, then took a sip of whatever he was drinking. But he took the money and the bag that Toni handed to him. "I hope you get some sleep tonight," he said.

"Good night," she said, then turned and reentered her house. She readied for bed, and before her eyes were completely closed, she dreamed of her daughter and the two grandbabies she had only heard rumors about.

Printed in the USA
CPSIA information can be obtained
at www.ICGtesting.com
CBHW051231150724
11315CB00003B/3